SUNDERED

*Brent,
Prepare to be
"Sundered!"
Best of Luck
Natasha Marusja*

SUNDERED

NATASHIA MORRISSEY

TATE PUBLISHING
AND ENTERPRISES, LLC

Sundered
Copyright © 2015 by Natashia Morrissey. All rights reserved.

No part of this publication may be reproduced, stored in a retrieval system or transmitted in any way by any means, electronic, mechanical, photocopy, recording or otherwise without the prior permission of the author except as provided by USA copyright law.

The opinions expressed by the author are not necessarily those of Tate Publishing, LLC.

This novel is a work of fiction. Names, descriptions, entities, and incidents included in the story are products of the author's imagination. Any resemblance to actual persons, events, and entities is entirely coincidental.

Published by Tate Publishing & Enterprises, LLC
127 E. Trade Center Terrace | Mustang, Oklahoma 73064 USA
1.888.361.9473 | www.tatepublishing.com

Tate Publishing is committed to excellence in the publishing industry. The company reflects the philosophy established by the founders, based on Psalm 68:11,
"The Lord gave the word and great was the company of those who published it."

Book design copyright © 2015 by Tate Publishing, LLC. All rights reserved.
Cover design by Ian Hiroto Mayhew
Interior design by Jomel Pepito

Published in the United States of America
ISBN: 978-1-63449-922-4
1. Fiction / Action & Adventure
2. Fiction / Dystopian
15.01.02

1

"Good morning, citizens of Sunderi! I am Brett Varmes, here to present to you the daily news. Today is July 3, 2197, and as you may have already heard this morning, SGPs have found another illegal operation underway. No one is to be alarmed. The SGPs are just doing their regular routine sweeps. Everything is being taken care of. Again, no one is to be alarmed."

Jonathon Richtor lifted his head from his desk, where he was reading, to watch the TV. He watched as the unfriendly-looking reporter continued to stare blankly forward, his eyes devoid of all possible emotion.

"On further news, the economy has had a 6 percent climb, further erasing prior debt the country has had. Up next, we'll be discussing possible changes to come! Until then, stay tuned."

Jonathon scoffed. Every day a similar message was broadcasted from the same reporter giving the same blank expression. "Don't worry, the SGPs—Security Grafted Personnel—won't harm you as they're too busy looking for bootleggers, delinquents, and every other miscreant who ever existed. There's no need for alarm. The building that was blown up today was just an abandoned house. Stay tuned as we cover the heroic efforts of our very own SGPs who took down a drug cartel today." Despite the false reports that the news was fond of telling every day, Jonathon had continued to watch the news out of pure habit.

Natashia Morrissey

In the past, Jonathon Richtor had been an astonishing field reporter who had a natural talent for getting even the best-kept secrets uncovered. Being 6"4', 160 pounds, with short strawberry-blonde hair and striking green eyes, he had no problem getting people to talk—everyone, from the local police officers to the next dirty politician who was desperate to knock his competition out of the running. He was truly unrivaled. That was until a certain case caused the biggest fiasco of his career and rendered him disgraced.

Jonathon returned his attention to his desk. On his desk, he had various papers skewed about, each covered in colorful sticky notes. In front of him, he had his contacts list he was previously pouring over a marble ashtray and a pack of Dusty Picks cigarettes. Dusty Picks was a bad lifelong habit for Jonathon. He had become addicted to them when he was a teenager, a decision that he regretted to this day. The cinnamon-flavored menthol was what hooked him and will probably keep him hooked until the day he died.

Pushing the contacts list aside, Jonathon pulled a cigarette out of the pack and lighted it. He took a long drag on it and then slowly closed his eyes, savoring the cinnamon flavor that burned down his throat. When he was done savoring the first puff, he opened his eyes just as the news was playing its next segment of the promised changes to come.

"Every day it's the same old nonsense," Jonathon said before taking another drag.

"You don't say?" said a voice behind him.

Jonathon turned around to see his younger sister, Madison, lying on the La-Z-Boy across the TV. She had shoulder-length strawberry-blonde hair and the same green eyes that the rest of the family shared. Her features were mostly delicate, but it was hard to tell these days with her complexion. It seemed every week she was losing more and more weight. Madison had been sick over half her life. At fourteen, she had been diagnosed with an unidentified autoimmune disease. Jonathon had been the one to care for her and his son at the time after the untimely death of their parents. So far, they've been able to make due with her illness, but most recently, they had run out of medication. With the state of the world as it was then, medications or any other resource outside of food was difficult to come by.

Jonathon put his cigarette out in the marble ashtray before picking up a blanket from the end table located next to his desk. He made sure the air-purifier system in the underground apartment was still working smoothly before bringing the blanket over to Madison and laying it on top of her. Madison had her eyes closed and arms wrapped tightly around her tiny torso as if she was cold.

"These announcements they're doing is just their way of saying 'Hey, we're on another kill streak. Better run before we get you!'" Jonathon grimaced. "The last one they did, we barely got you out of that hospital before they blew it up."

"Yeah, and as thankful as I am for you saving me, there are some days when I wish I had blown up too. My body aches, Jon, and if I can't get treatment soon, then I'm as good as dead."

"I know, Maddie. I'm looking. I'm trying to pull every resource I can to find a doctor who can get you the help and meds you need." He strode across the room back to his desk chair. "And I know you'll try to say that you're better at this than I am, and you might be right. However, we have no access to a computer for you to use and search."

"Are you sure you've ex-ex-exhausted all your sources for a computer?" Madison's teeth chattered as she squirmed under the blanket trying to keep warm.

Jonathon ran his hands through his hair, trying to rack his brain to see if there was any other source he could think of. After drawing a blank, he reached across the desk to where a stack of books was piled. He began opening each and every one of them, looking through all the contacts and informants. He had X'd almost every single person he had listed whom he had contacted over the past couple months and to no avail. And many times, he had gone over the same list repeatedly, hoping he had just missed someone. Each time he felt more and more despair.

Today, however, he noticed there was a name on his list that did not have an X.

X ~~Source: Claire Williams~~
X ~~Info: Roger Tullip~~
Info: River Rutherford
X ~~Source: Michael Douglas~~

In fact, staring at it, he couldn't figure out why he never noticed it before. Then it hit him. River Rutherford was his inside informant for the government. Her father, Arthur Rutherford, was the chairman for the Council of Economic Advisors and was always looking for ways to pad his pockets. Surely if he could get ahold of River, she could get help for Madison.

Jonathon paced for a while, trying to figure out how he was going to get ahold of River. He couldn't take Madison with him because of how sick she was getting. But he also didn't want to leave her here in his underground apartment all by herself. He groaned at the realization that he would need to move her to a safe location where someone could watch over her in his absence. Sadly, there was no one even remotely close by.

He turned to look at Madison just as she began to burst into a fit of heavy coughs. He knelt down in front of her and held her hands, trying to comfort her. Her tiny body shook as she tried to regain control of her breathing. When she finally got her breathing under control, Jonathon got up and poured her a glass of water.

"Thank you," Madison said before she started drinking slowly.
"It's getting worse…"
"I know. I can feel it."

Sundered

Jonathon raised his hands to his head and ran them through his hair. *It seems I have no choice but to move her*, he thought. *The question is—where and how?*

2

River, using her hand to push her stark-blue hair out of her eyes, moved her head around the corner. Seven SGPs were scouting the area still looking for her. *Shit. This might be a bit of a challenge to get back*, she thought. She looked down at the bullet wound in her leg, trying to determine if she was going to be able to run on it or not.

I probably could, but not for long.

She still couldn't believe that bullet had ricocheted off the metal beam and hit her as she was running for cover. *Better clean it and wrap it before I even attempt this.* She groaned.

Pulling off her backpack, she reached for the gauze and antiseptic she had in the front pocket. She breathed in deep and winced, trying desperately to stay as quiet as possible while she poured the antiseptic over the bullet wound. She cringed as she felt the burn seep deeply into the wound. She heard footsteps as she began to hastily wrap the gauze around her leg. She peeked around the corner again from where she was hiding. The SGPs were moving toward her position.

"This is bad," she said to herself. *I've got no choice but to make a mad dash and hopefully get out of their sight, all while on a bummed leg.* She scanned her surroundings, looking for another place to hide. There was nothing close by. The only thing she could think of was the ravine; however, that was over two hundred feet to the east. *No choice. I'm going to have to risk it,* she thought as she climbed to her feet.

River took off running carefully, trying to zigzag as adrenaline poured through her entire body. She slid trying to step around the debris and instinctively threw her head forward as a bullet whistled right above her head. She dove forward to get out of sight then got right back up and broke out in a dead run back toward the ravine.

Less than a hundred feet to go, I can do this.

Bullets were flying past her, causing the adrenaline in her body to course faster and faster. Up ahead she noticed a boulder large enough for her to hide behind, not twenty feet from the ravine. River dove forward and continued to roll until she got behind it. Gunfire continued all around and behind her. She could feel her heartbeat in her throat as she looked over at the edge. She leaned forward trying to get a better look. She could see the bottom.

Okay, this won't be too bad, she thought. *Here goes!*

River ran forward and jumped into the ravine, landing on her feet and then down to a knee. Her leg was screaming pain all over. Blood gushed out, soaking the gauze. She bit down on her hand to try to prevent herself from screaming.

Can't stay here. I gotta keep moving. She panted.

River struggled as she tried to stand, but the pain in her leg made it impossible. Bracing herself, she raised herself on one leg and began hopping on it. She made it a couple feet before she had to stop. *I cannot hop the rest of the way back,* she thought as she put her other leg to the ground. The pain was still excruciating, but she was slowly getting used to it. *Maybe I can make it the rest of the way.* She took a step forward. Pain still shot up her leg.

Shots and voices rang out behind her again. The SGPs were closing in on her.

River put the side of her hand in between her teeth and bit down as she staggered forward. Before reaching the end of her endurance, she traveled inside, looking for the gate console. She spotted it nearby and began to immediately open the interface, in hopes of trying to close the gate. Error after error popped up as she grew increasingly frustrated and panicked. She could hear loud stomping and shouts closing in from outside the gate.

Fed up, she shoved her right fist into the console and created her own interface inside her head. Within ten seconds, the word *granted* sprawled across her vision, and the large gate slammed shut with a loud thud.

3

"How are you holding up, Maddie?" Jon asked as he looked over at her in the passenger seat.

"So far, so good. Can't complain, but can't really say I like the entertainment." Madison turned her head toward the window and made a face. "The scenery sucks too."

Jon chuckled as he continued to steer his Land Rover. The Land Rover was the first thing he and his now ex-wife bought together. Back then, he thought it was the craziest thing he'd ever seen with an even crazier price tag, but somehow, Deborah convinced him it was a great find, saying that eventually it would pay for itself. It didn't back then as it did little else except sit in the garage as work continued to increase and grow with the years churning forward. But in the last ten years, Jon was convinced he wouldn't have been able to survive without it, let alone keep Maddie safe.

"Hey, what are you daydreaming about over there?"

Jon looked back over at Madison staring up at him. "Nothing. Sorry for staring off into space like that." He patted her head, smiling as he did so. "Just trying to remember the safest way to Claire's, that's all."

Madison scowled and shifted in her seat, muttering something under her breath.

"I don't have anywhere else you can hide safely. Plus, I know Claire can watch you while I'm trying to get you the meds you need."

Madison looked out the window again. "She's not the one I have an issue with. It's her cowardice excuse for a husband that's the problem."

"Brad's… something else that's for sure… but he's got some admirable qualities somewhere. Why else would Claire stay married to him?"

Madison shifted in her seat again and looked at Jonathon. "She doesn't stay with him because of his qualities. She stays with him because he's an excuse." She sighed heavily as she turned her head to look out the windshield. "Don't get me wrong, Jon. I love Claire. She's our sister after all…but she's changed. It's like she's no longer the same person."

Jonathon looked over at Madison briefly before returning his gaze to the road that lay before them. While it was true that Claire had changed tremendously, it wasn't without good reason. Jonathon scanned the horizon looking for the familiar landmarks that let him know he was getting close. He spotted the broken down thrift store Tendies before long and made a right turn to continue on the road. After an extended period of silence in the SUV, Jonathon decided that it wasn't his place and that if Madison really wanted to know what happened to Claire, then she would have to asked Claire on her own accord.

"How much longer do we have to go?" Madison asked, yawning. A small fit of coughs followed afterward as she placed a hand in front of her face. Jonathon took his eyes away from the road long enough to place his hand on her back before moving it back and forth in a soothing manner. When she finished coughing, she closed her eyes and lay back in the seat.

"Shouldn't be much longer…I believe we're only twenty minutes away," Jonathon responded before making a right turn.

Sundered

The landscape that lay before them was rather metallic in color. A silver sky stretched out over the roads that were constantly being paved by the maintenance droids each week, even though very little traffic came upon them. Lights were in constant perfect working order, maintained by small generators that were buried beneath each of them. Everywhere you traveled, drove, or climbed upon was in perfect order, as if nothing was wrong in the world. Grocery stores, hospitals, schools, and auto shops were still operable even though none of them saw people or customers.

Over a decade ago, the economy of Sunderi, our whole planet, was on the verge of collapsing from the depression. The government went through great lengths to try to relieve the economic deficit, but no matter what they tried, nothing worked. More deficit was accumulated, more jobs were lost, and every day more and more people were living on the streets. One day, it seemed as if the entire government had given up and just disappeared. A few years later, they finally made another appearance. They claimed they had been hard at work and had discovered a foolproof plan for the deficit that was rapidly eating away at our world. They called the plan Economic Relief and were going to put it into effect as soon as possible. Little did we know of the terror that would shortly follow.

It started with five of the officials being jailed. Then the remaining thirteen officials who made up the rest of the cabinet started recruiting, conditioning, and microchipping mercenaries. These microchips rendered the mercenaries unable to question authority and removed all free thought. They created several designated kill lists that included everyone from the disabled to the greedy CEOs who spent lavishly. The lists stated that all "unfit" individuals were to be killed or buried alive. Shortly afterward, they sent out a mass broadcast across all media outlets stating that changes were about to be made. Then all became dark.

First to go was the government welfare list. Second were the individuals who had been on unemployment for excessive periods of time. Third were corrupt police officers who were taking advantage of their jobs. The government then set out a list to every CEO in the country informing them that they were required to change their policies and conditions or otherwise they would be forced to eliminate them. Only twenty-three CEOs still stood today after correctly abiding by the list they were given. The rest were completely eradicated after they tried to send large sums of cash to the government, requesting that they shouldn't have to. Over time, government started taking out every little group that either caused an economic disturbance or deficit until only a third of the population was left. The government succeeded in fixing the economic deficit like they said they would—but the massacre didn't stop there. Every once in a while, the government officials would still send out more mercenaries to demolish riots and free healthcare clinics. With the economy finally pulling out of the deficit, the population had become sundered.

Those who survived coined the last ten years as the Decade of Eradication. No one could figure out why the government thought that the other option they had was to kill as many people as they could. They never offered any explanation or condolences. As a matter of fact, none of them had been seen since the day the eradication started. Who knows if they're even still alive or not?

"We're finally here," Jonathon said as he pulled his Land Rover into a steel driveway hidden beneath a large willow tree. A green interface appeared on the driver-side window as he came to a stop. He pressed the intercom button and waited for a response. A few seconds later, a beautiful brunette appeared on the interface.

"Jonathon! Why, this is an unexpected surprise. What brings you here?" the lady asked.

"Hey, Claire, I apologize for this being last minute, but I need a favor. Normally I wouldn't make this type of call…but I honestly don't have a choice," he said to the screen.

Sundered

"I suppose I should let you in then," Claire replied. The driveway creaked and gave away as Claire gave permission for the Land Rover to enter.

4

"Oh, why did you have to let him in, Claire?" Brad asked, irritability sprawling across his face.

Claire turned away from the intercom system to look at her husband of the past fifteen years. Bradford Jameson stood six-feet tall with blue eyes and short light-brown hair. He never liked his full name and made it a point to always introduce himself as Brad. Claire eventually had asked him about it one day, and the only response he gave her was "It's because of my father." No real explanation at all.

Claire had met Brad long before the eradication, when she was still drag racing. He was a voice of reason and a shield when she needed it. However, on other occasions, he was overprotective and a pain in the ass.

"He's my brother, Brad. I'm not just going to turn him away on the account that you don't like him," she replied, opening the front door.

Claire walked outside just as the driveway had finished descending down the hydraulic lift. The hydraulic lift had been put in place long before the eradication began. It was a decision she had made in the middle of her career just after she came across Brad. As other drivers were constantly seeking out her cars, Brad and his company had approached her about setting up

Sundered

an underground car garage. They had installed six lifts at the time, of which only one was still working today.

Brad watched from the window as Claire and Jonathon exchanged handshakes and then hugs before a young lady emerged from the Land Rover. She was very thin and pale to the point that her hair was the only thing with color. It also matched Jonathon's hair. *Another relative perhaps?* Brad rubbed his chin as he contemplated Claire's family tree. He knew she had a brother who was Jonathon as he had altercations with him before. He and Jonathon had a habit of bumping heads all the time due to not only their professions but their personalities as well. Brad could briefly recall Claire having a sister but wasn't certain if the woman who arrived with Jonathon was her or not, let alone what her name was. Or if she was still alive for that matter.

Shaking his head, he turned away from the window just as Claire came through the front door.

"Brad? Don't you wanna come say hello?" Claire asked, her hand on the door. She noticed the scowl on his face and proceeded to walk over to him, wrapping her arms around his slender waist. Claire stared at him with her bright-green eyes, looking just as beautiful as she did the day he met her.

Brad sighed, pecked a kiss on her forehead, and pulled himself out of her hug to head for the door. He hated to admit it, but he couldn't help but melt every time she stared at him like that. It was as if she had this hypnotizing gaze that put him under a spell each and every time.

He met Jonathon at the door, the scowl still evident on his face.

"Bradford!" Jonathon shouted as his mouth shifted into a sly grin. He extended his hand out to Brad, a look of amusement gleaming in his eyes. Brad rolled his eyes as he took Jonathon's hand, returning the handshake.

"Jonathon," Brad replied sternly.

"Are you done tormenting him yet, Jon?" the pale woman spoke up, irritation in her voice.

Brad turned his gaze to the young woman. Up close, the pale woman appeared younger and at the same time extremely fragile, as if she could break at any moment. Yet there was a sense of fire from her that left Brad confused. He had sensed this particular fire only once before. And that was when he realized that the woman who stood in front him was Madison.

"Yo, Brad. You just gonna stand there all day staring?" Madison asked as she moved past him to lie on the couch.

"Madison?" Brad said in disbelief.

"In the flesh and colorless," she replied before exploding into a fit of coughs. She struggled to pull herself upright as she continued to cough, each one sounding worse than the last. Jonathon and Claire both rushed to her side to help her up. Madison continued to cough still. Jonathon began to rub her back.

"Claire, can you get her a glass of water? She'll need it once she stops," Jonathon asked, watching Madison carefully. Claire nodded and went into the next room. She returned a moment later just as Madison's coughs subsided.

Brad was still standing by the front door, unsure of what was going on. He watched as Claire handed Madison the glass of water, who thanked her before drinking from it slowly. *Is this sickly woman truly Madison? I know I've probably met her...what, twice, over a decade ago? But still...what the hell happened to her?* Brad shifted uncomfortably. *No no no. Why did Jonathon bring her here? Is he tired of watching over her? Does he just want to go out and wander? Although in this day and age...it's practically impossible with the government as shitty as it is.*

"Honey, come sit down. You don't have to keep standing by the door," Claire said, her bright green eyes staring at him again.

"Yeah, come sit next to me. I don't bite...hard." Jonathon flashed another sly grin at Brad.

Instant annoyance flooded into Brad's face, and he muttered under his breath. He closed the door, crossed the room to the recliner, which was located diagonally to the couch, and sat down. For one reason or another, Jonathon always found a way to get under Brad's skin, intentionally and otherwise. And being the man that he was, Brad could never hold in his irritation or annoyance and turned to Jonathon.

"What the hell are you doing here, Jonathon? Are you dragging us into another one of your schemes? If you are, you better leave now."

The amusement drained away from Jonathon's face, and he stared hard at Brad. His eyes, while they were the same color as Claire's, had turned both cold and angry. "If I had another option, I wouldn't have even bothered coming here. I'm fully capable of taking care of her, no thanks to you."

"What's this all about, Jon?" Claire asked softly, looking back and forth between him and Madison.

Jonathon sighed heavily. "Maddie's about out of her meds, and I need someone to watch her while I go get more." Jonathon paused briefly before continuing on. "In the past, I've taken Maddie with me whenever I go to get her medication, but unfortunately, with the sharp increase in the SGPs' activities, it's much too risky and dangerous to take her along."

"Is this why she looks so god awful?" Brad asked bluntly while pointing at Madison. "Wait a minute, why would you wait until practically the last minute to get her medication if she needs it so badly?" He slowly started to rise from the recliner. "This sounds like too much of an excuse. Get out of here. Go find someone else to manipulate!"

"Brad, sit down and shut up!" Claire stared at her husband sternly. "Jonathon may be a lot of things…but I know for a fact he would never do anything intentionally to hurt our family. Matter of fact, he's the one who stepped up to the plate to raise Maddie after our parents were killed. He never asked for any help and always took care of her even when she fell sick." She turned to look at Madison. "Which I'm going to assume, you still haven't recovered from that illness?"

Madison nodded.

"You poor thing…if Jonathon believes it's too dangerous to take you along, then I believe him. You can stay here with us, Maddie, until Jon can get you your meds."

"Thank you, Claire…truly thank you."

Jonathon breathed a sigh of relief. *Finally I can get her what she needs to feel better and not have to worry about who's going to watch her.*

"Jon? When's the last time she had a scan done?"

Jonathon thought for a moment and blew out air. "Well, she had one done about six months ago when I was able to track down a hospital that wasn't under SGP jurisdiction. However, before we could review the results, we had to evacuate the building immediately as the hospital had obtained Intel warning about an incoming SGP bombing. And trust me…if that Intel was any later, none of us would have made it out of that hospital alive."

Claire hesitated for a moment and afterward reached under the tabletop and pulled out what appeared to be a handheld scanning device. Madison stared at the device, a look of confusion appearing on her face. It changed to a look of relief a minute later.

"You know what this is, Maddie?" Claire asked, noticing her facial change.

Madison nodded. "It's a hol-hol-holographic body scanner. You use it to scan the entire length of a body to get a full 4D print." She paused for a moment as curiosity washed over her. "Why do you have one?"

"That's…a story I will tell another time. For now, I want to examine you so I can get a better understanding of what's afflicting you."

Claire pressed a few buttons on the top of the scanner, causing it to turn on and open its interactive interface. To verify it worked properly, she placed her left hand in front of it and watched as it rapidly began to accumulate information and a full 4D hologram of her hand. Satisfied with the detailed analysis and image it produced, Claire motioned for Madison to stand up straight.

"This won't hurt, Madison, but try not to move as I scan over your entire body. Shouldn't be too long."

5

"My god, this is...how?"

"Given our little apartment wasn't the greatest in terms of sterility, I've wondered the same thing several times."

"This should be impossible...I mean, you're trying to tell me she's had this for the past ten years? What the hell were in those pills?"

Madison eyes fluttered opened, and the overwhelming urge to vomit caused her to sit up right on the couch just long enough for her to put her head between her legs. Jonathon's and Claire's voices soon shuffled into the room as they heard Madison dry heaving.

"Maddie! Claire, quick! Get some bread and a bowl." Jonathon sat next to Madison on the couch and pulled her hair away from her face.

A few more minutes passed before Madison managed to stop dry heaving. Sitting back, breathing somewhat heavily, she reached for Jonathon's hand and attempted to squeeze it. She couldn't. Jonathon looked at her and then to their hands before frowning. He was beginning to feel even more uneasy about leaving her here while he went to get her medication. But he reminded himself that if he didn't get the medication, then Madison could very well die.

Claire entered the room with the requested bread and bowl. She placed the bowl on the coffee table in front of the couch and then proceeded to hand Madison a slice of bread from the loaf. Madison popped pieces of the slice into her mouth, doing her best to fight the next wave of nausea. Her whole body ached, and the muscles in her stomach twisted and pulled as she forced herself to eat the slice Claire handed her and two more.

Jonathon paced around the room. The familiar sense of dread was beginning to take hold, and he wondered once more if he should just risk taking Madison with him. As if sensing his discomfort, Claire looked at him. "Don't worry, Jon. I can take care of Maddie. I should have enough experience as a nurse to be able to keep her fed and comfortable until you get back, not to mention catch up and keep her company."

Jonathon looked over at Madison. As she sat there in discomfort on the couch slowly eating a piece of bread, memories of when he had to tell her their parents had gotten in a car crash came flooding back. Madison had just turned six, and she looked so sad and confused. Jonathon had driven all three of them—Claire, Madison, and himself—to the hospital to check on their condition. While the circumstances and details as to why the accident occurred were sketchy, the bodies of Dennis and Renee Richtor told a different story. The police investigated the car crash for a while, but nothing turned up. Jonathon himself attempted to look into the matter as something about it just didn't sit right with him. Unfortunately, nothing ever came up.

Nodding, Jonathon turned away from the two of them and moved toward the door. Breathing out heavily, he took one last glance at Madison. For the first time in eighteen years, she was being cared for by someone else. Steeling his nerves, he walked out the door.

6

River stopped and leaned against the sewer walls, breathing heavily. After cutting off the SGPs route to her, River had found a sewer channel access within the fort and had been making her way through it ever since. The sewers were pungent and smelled of death, decay, and vomit. She had already stopped twice while traveling through the sewers to throw up as the air left an almost constant aftertaste in her mouth. But still she pressed on, adamant as ever, despite the nausea rumbling in her system.

The air was becoming harsher on her lungs, and the pain in her right leg was finally evolving into a very painful numbing sensation. It was like every nerve within her leg was on fire and seemed to reignite with every step she took. She slid down the sewer wall and extended her legs in front of her. Her bandages were completely soaked and caked in blood, dirt, and grime. She would need to change them out before moving again to avoid an infection spreading. She took a moment to breathe, trying her best to block out the smells of the sewer before leaning forward to take off her backpack.

Inside her backpack, she had half a bottle of antiseptic, two more rolls of bandages, a pair of tweezers, a flare, and a gun. *A gun? When did this get in here?* She picked up the gun and began to look it over. It was a Sig Sauer P226 modified with a laser sight, silencer, and a longer handle to accommodate a larger ammunition clip. The serial number was filed off, and in its place, the initials XF40 stood. *Xavier…you snuck this in my bag before I left. I wish I had realized this was in here earlier. Probably wouldn't be in the predicament I'm in now.* Releasing the clip, she checked to see how many rounds she had. Thirty-nine bullets gleamed back at her. *Well, getting back will be easier now in case I run into more of them. How the hell did I not notice this earlier when I was bandaging the first time?* She stared closer at the clip. What she thought was a thirty-nine round clip was actually forty. One bullet was missing.

Not thinking much about it, River slid the magazine back into the handle. Setting the gun aside, she reached forward and began to unwrap the blood-and-grime–soaked bandages around her shin. The skin all around the bullet wound was already turning shades of yellow and purple. The bullet wound in itself looked incredibly angry, and another layer of pus was beginning to form at the site. An infection was already setting into her leg. River groaned loudly at her luck. At this point, she needed to get back to the base faster than before if she wanted any chance of avoiding gangrene.

River grabbed the bottle of antiseptic and braced herself before pouring its remaining contents all over the bullet wound. She thought the searing pains she felt before were excruciating. That pain magnified itself when it became coupled with the sharp sensation of the antiseptic bubbling over the wound. It was more than enough to cause her to jump up to her feet, but not for long as the pain caused her to fall back down to her knees. Unable to block out the sickening smell within the sewers, River started vomiting profusely, and before long, the only thing coming up was blood.

Several minutes passed before she could collect her bearings. She placed a hand over her mouth and raised herself upright. Despite the sewer being the smelliest place she'd ever ventured into, it was not the worst place she'd ever been or even the most dangerous. Closing her eyes, she steeled herself by breathing in deep and concentrating on her right arm. The tolerance for the putrid smells of the sewer came back, and a feeling of relief flooded over her. River picked up her backpack and zipped it close before flinging it over her shoulders. She picked up the Sig from where she had set it on the floor and proceeded to make her way through the rest of the sewer.

River made it out of the sewer an hour later. The sewer tunnel she was traveling through ended at the Silent drain field. Silent drain field was a lesser-known drain field that ran partially aboveground and underground into a reservoir where it was completely filtered into freshwater. To this day, River still had no idea how the machinery inside the reservoir was able to filter the sewer water so cleanly. And after experiencing the sewer water firsthand today, she was ever thankful that this particular piece of technology had survived the government massacre.

Battered and shivering from the cold breezes blowing over the drain field, River picked up her pace in an effort to keep warm. From Silent drain field, it would only take her forty-five minutes to find one of the five entrances into Axler. Axler was the name Xavier had given to their base of operations; he constructed five sets of tunnel systems around it. Each one of the tunnel systems had entrances into various environments and were very carefully hidden. It's without saying that unless you know exactly what you're looking for, the chances of you finding the entrances into the tunnel systems are slim to none.

The remainder of River's trip back to the base was slow and uneventful. She located the regular-looking rock and felt along the middle of it to twist it until a key shape appeared among its side. The key rock was then inserted into an inconspicuous looking knot on one of the solo trees in the area. A soft click followed afterward, and a section of the ground around the tree sank in before sliding back to reveal a ladder leading into the tunnel system River was looking for. Before climbing down the ladder, River twisted the key rock back around and placed it back down on the ground. After climbing down the ladder and reaching the first landing, River punched in the three-digit code into the security panel to close the entrance. She then continued along the landing to the flight of stairs, which went down to the second landing, and staggered her way to the main room of the base.

It was there that Xavier Frost was waiting for her. An obvious look of relief flooded over River's face before she collapsed to the floor and passed out.

7

Jonathon watched from the top of the hill with his binoculars as a battalion of SGPs marched across the countryside. He flicked two switches on inside his Land Rover and continued to watch the SGPs' movements until his dashboard console slid down to reveal a geothermal 3D layout of the surrounding area. Putting his binoculars down, he moved his eyes along the map, looking for a path that wasn't populated with the silent but menacing mercenaries. As John flicked another switch, the radio came on, and a stoic voice filled the cabin.

"Reports show the Settler's Camp is attempting to descend upon our beloved city. Our SGPs have been dispatched to the area in an attempt to thwart their nefarious plan. National security has requested for everyone to take refuge inside their houses to avoid being caught in the crossfires."

Jonathon raised an eyebrow at the broadcast and then used his binoculars to look back at the battalion. Nothing resembling the Settler's Camp caravan or its members was anywhere to be seen. As a matter of fact, the SGPs were still just marching across the field, their MP5s thumping against the sides of their legs. As the radio started to repeat its initial broadcast, Jonathon put his binoculars on the passenger seat, lit up a cigarette, and then put the Land Rover into drive. He drove back down the hill and

Sundered

onto the perfectly paved road where numerous serviceroids were meticulously cleaning the streetlights.

The serviceroids were robots that looked partially humanoid and suddenly appeared during the eradication. Jonathon theorized that it had to have been the government that commissioned them, but he couldn't figure out why exactly. There was hardly any human life left, and those who are left try to avoid traveling during the day. And yet the serviceroids were deployed daily to clean the streets and the capital city.

He maneuvered around them, scoffing. Glancing at the geothermal display, he noticed that each of the serviceroids glowed dark red. According to the meter, each serviceroid was generating enough heat to warm a small mansion. Jonathon pondered briefly whether or not the serviceroid would blow up if he were to hit one with his vehicle. Driving along, he passed by thirty more serviceroids, each doing the same thing as the last. One briefly stopped cleaning and seemed to dart out in front of his vehicle but instead stopped to clear away some debris that was piling up on the curb. Jonathon had to stop for a brief moment to recover from the miniature heartache this gave him before he could continue on.

An unusual geothermal reading came up on the display about fifteen miles away. Based on the spacing between the heat sources, Jonathon speculated he was coming up on a group of people. *The Settler's Camp?* There was only slight movement in between the various heat sources. *Doesn't look like they're staging an attack to me.* Stopping the vehicle on the side of the road, he grabbed his binoculars.

Ahead of him on the horizon was not just a group of people. It was an entire caravan settlement. Jonathon had found the new location for the Settler's Camp. He had run into them once or twice in the years past as they were constantly moving around. While most of the survivors decided that living underground was the best way of getting away from the SGPs, the people of the Settler's Camp traveled nomadically aboveground and went on what they called *kelco* from time to time to reduce the SGPs numbers.

Knowing the SGPs were soon going to be in the vicinity, Jonathon drove onward toward the caravan. Looking around, Jonathon noticed there were a number of metal scraps and body parts on both sides of the road. Blood and scorch marks were everywhere, making the surrounding area look like one hell of a warzone. Jonathon took a second look at the scrap metal and realized the pieces of scrap that littered the area were from serviceroids. Judging from the patterns of the scorch marks, it looked like the serviceroids had been catapulted into the previously advancing SGPs. And as irony would have it, there was a lone serviceroid fully functional in the middle of the entire mess, doing its best to clean up the carnage. Jonathon couldn't stop laughing and almost dropped his cigarette.

He arrived at the entrance of the Settler's Camp not two minutes later and was met by two hunters. Jonathon recognized one of them but wondered if the guy still remembered him after four years. He was 6"2', 180 pounds easy, dark-skinned, and ripped with muscles. Jonathon remembered him as George Lemsky, but for reasons unknown to him, the other hunter called him Tiny George.

"Richtor?" Tiny George asked, an eyebrow arched.

"Lemsky," Jonathon responded, a little relieved that the giant had remembered him. That relief almost instantly turned into panic as Tiny George picked him up by the middle suddenly and squeezed him tight. His face started to turn blue, and he tried to claw Tiny George's back to get his attention. It did not work.

"Easy now, Tiny, you're squeezing all his air out," the other hunter said, chuckling.

"Oooh sorry!" Tiny George exclaimed before releasing Jonathon.

Jonathon fell flat on the floor, gasping for air. Tiny George picked him up by one arm and placed him on his feet. Jonathon struggled to catch his breath for a few minutes as he kept looking back and forth between Tiny George and the other hunter. The other hunter caught his eyes a couple times and, as if reading his mind, proceeded to speak.

"I'm Randall Jamesson. But you can call me RJ." The other hunter stuck out his hand. Jonathon returned the handshake and took a hard look at his face. Randall had some subtle similarities to someone else he knew. The only difference was this man was much taller—and manlier.

"Jamesson...are you...by any chance...related to Brad...Jamesson?" Jonathon asked in between breaths.

"He's my younger cousin." RJ looked surprised. "How do you know him?"

"Oh...he's married to one of my sisters." Jonathon let out a long breath.

"Hah! Old sourpuss actually got married? When? Couldn't have been during the eradication, could it?" RJ laughed. "Knowing him, it could have been. Wait...is he still alive?"

"Yeah, he's still kicking, no worries there. Brad and Claire have been married...ooooh fifteen years now, I think? Yeah, fifteen sounds about right. I'm afraid he's never liked me though." Jonathon flashed a smile.

"I can see why. Although I might be wrong. He's always had a bad jealous streak, and with your good looks, I'm sure that only added fuel to the fire."

"He's married to my sister. What the hell could he possibly be jealous of me over?"

"I can't quite tell you the story since it's not my place to say anything, but let's just say...some of the weirdest things have happened to that guy."

"Like what? A brother and sister running off together?" Jonathon said, trying to crack a joke.

RJ looked around, twiddling his thumbs. Jonathon grimaced.

"Since the cat is out of the bag now…" RJ started to stare at the sky. "There was a girl he was absolutely head over heels for. But as you guessed, she ended up running off with her brother. Her whole family had problems, and we tried telling Brad over and over again to leave them alone, but he wouldn't listen. Eventually, the chick's brother ended up tying him to a tree. We didn't find him until two days later." RJ looked over at Jonathon. "As you can imagine, he was livid."

"That does explain a few things. However… listen, RJ…"

"And then there was this time with this other crazy chick. Oh boy, the things I can tell you about that—"

"That's great, RJ, but there's something else I need to ask you about—"

"She used to take these stems and place them between her teeth and then—"

"RANDY!" Jonathon cut him off again.

Tiny George began to laugh as RJ continued to ramble. Jonathon almost forgot Tiny George was still standing there. He turned his attention to him.

"I'm looking for any information you guys have on either River Rutherford or where I can get some hard to find medications. Is there someone within the caravan who can direct me to either, George?"

Tiny George nodded. "River's one of the security couriers and helps us get certain supplies from time to time. She should be able to help you find what you need. If not, you could always try asking our leader, Glorious Fish."

"Glorious Fish?" Jonathon looked dubious.

Tiny George chuckled and nodded again.

"Should I ask?"

"You'll know why once you see her," RJ responded, coming into their conversation. Sadly, he didn't realize nobody was listening to him rambling until they had turned their backs to him.

Sundered

Jonathon nodded despite not knowing exactly what they meant. He shook hands with both RJ and Tiny George as they pointed him in the direction of Glorious Fish. As he was turning away, another question popped into his head. "Hey, Lemsky?"

"Yes, Richtor?" Tiny George turned his back toward him.

"So quick question...when did you become *Tiny* George?"

Tiny George started to change a shade of red.

"It's because his pecs are smaller than everyone else is in the caravan." RJ had once again jumped into the conversation.

Jonathon looked from Tiny George to RJ to some of the other hunters who were roaming around their caravan. Now that it had been pointed, it was very obvious that compared to everyone else there, Tiny George was indeed tiny. It could not have been good for his ego.

Tiny George shot RJ a look, and RJ began to chuckle before clapping his hand down on Tiny George's shoulder, muttering a few words of inspiration before they both turned and walked away.

Jonathon stood there wondering for a little while what exactly was going to be in store for him when he met the Glorious Fish. RJ said she was female. As he stood and pondered on it more, he remembered a report he had once intercepted from the SGPs that spoke of a woman leading a group of thirty individuals against the battalion of three hundred SGPs. According to the report, the entire battalion of SGPs had been ambushed, and more than half of the bodies went missing.

With this in mind, Jonathon pulled out his pack of Dusty Picks and lit a cigarette. It had been too long since he was able to smoke so freely and even more so in open air. He counted his remaining cigarettes—4 were left—and made a mental note for himself to check to see if they carried his brand within the Settler's Camp. For now, he puffed on his cigarette and prepared himself to meet Glorious Fish, anxious and excited to see if this was the same woman mentioned in the SGPs' report.

8

Xavier Frost hummed back and forth around the small room waiting for River to awake. Various gadgets and machines encompassed the room, each emitting their own sounds of beeps and whirls. Most of everything in this room was created by Xavier himself. Standing at 6"1', 184 pounds, with hazel eyes and long salt-and-pepper hair, he was an odd definition of engineer and scientist. At the age of thirty-three, he had obtained his masters in theoretical engineering and began an emphasis in human construction. Xavier was a brilliant creator in his own field. However, in his own way, he was also insane. Never satisfied with what he accomplished, he always set out to do something else once he finished.

    Due to the government's activities, Xavier was forced to go on the run to avoid being another checkmark on the designated kill lists. At the age of thirty-five twelve years ago, he had managed to create an entire new line of prosthetics that opened a whole new level of development for science and engineering. The funding required to keep that project going was what caught the government's attention. Xavier was the father of XF Prosthetics, prosthetics that were so articulate and well-balanced, it was like having your original organic limb. It was because of his prosthetics that he met River.

Sundered

She had pleaded with him to give her an arm after she was forced to cut off her own after the SGPs implanted her with a tracking device. A tracking device that would have traveled through her bloodstream until it reached her heart and then it would be impossible to remove without killing her. Xavier still remembered installing her prosthetic and the events that took place shortly afterward. He had barely finished linking up the actuators to her nervous system before the SGPs busted in, and River sprung off the table so fast, it was like she could float. She took the first SGP by surprise, stole his MP5, and proceeded to dart around the lobby area, taking out the rest of the squadron that had entered with the first. It was because of that they had decided to become partners.

Xavier stopped pacing in front of the painkillers monitor and made a few adjustments to lower the amount being administered into River's bloodstream. She was going to need to wake up sooner than later, and she was going to need to deal with the fact that he installed another prosthetic on her after she had passed out. He didn't have much choice, seeing how much blood had been lost and the amount of infection that was already starting to spread across her leg. It was a miracle she had walked on it as much as she had.

But knowing River, it was because she was stubborn and determined to get back, no matter what the odds were or how much pain she was in. She was definitely a fighter. She was also incredibly frightening when she was pissed off. Despite being only 5"6', she had a demeanor that made her seem like she was a giant. Deciding it would be best if she didn't see him as she woke up, Xavier left the room. Not more than ten minutes later, she awoke.

Blinking, she looked around the room. She was safely in Axler's recovery room. Breathing a sigh of relief, she ran her fingers through her short blue hair. It had been almost seven months since she last left Axler, and with each mission she assigned herself, her stays away from "home" were becoming longer and longer. Shaking her head, River tossed off the sheets covering her body and turned to slide off the hospital bed. As her feet hit the floor, she heard a metallic thud. She looked down. A metallic prosthetic was now in place of her previously bullet-struck leg.

River let out a scream. She leaned back on the bed trying to calm herself down. *There has to be a good reason why he couldn't save my leg.* Her mind instantly thought of the sewers. *Oh…I guess there's a pretty good chance that the infection spread faster than I thought it would.* Sticking her new prosthetic out in front of her, she was impressed with the weight of it. It was light and responded to every impulse she could think of. She placed her prosthetic back onto the floor and raised the other leg straight out in front of her. Even though she was happy with how easily it responded to her every whim, she wanted to make sure she would be able to depend on it. She began to dip slowly before shifting her body around into various fighting stances and yoga poses, testing to see how well the prosthetic could hold up with supporting her weight. She noticed no strains, grinds, or delayed reactions from her mechanical leg.

Satisfied with her impromptu tests, she walked across the recovery room to the intercom system stationed next to the door. Before she could press the button to call for Xavier, a voice began to boom from it.

"Good Morning, River."

"I see you've wasted no time on experimenting on me again in my sleep, Xavier."

A short silence followed before Xavier responded again. "I swear…this time, I really didn't have a choice. I'm not certain what you picked up from wherever you were traveling, but you had one hell of an infection that was spreading at an alarming rate. It was either cut off your leg or watch you die an increasingly

Sundered

painful death." He paused for a moment before adding, "I believe I told you good morning."

"Yeah, yeah, good morning to you too. Listen, where are you right now?"

"I'm in my lab, tinkering at my next project. No, you're not allowed in."

River rolled her eyes. "So you don't want to hear how I was shot?" Thinking it was going to take a while to respond, she leaned against the wall. Surprisingly enough, he answered right away instead.

"I know how you were shot," he said, laughing. "You shot yourself. Why you would do that, I have no idea."

"I did not shoot myself, Xavier. I got hit by a stray ricochet while running from the SGPs. They caught me a little off guard…"

"River, come on. I did attempt to save your leg before making the decision to amputate. The bullet I removed from your leg belonged to the Sig I placed in your backpack before you left. You're losing your touch."

"Gee, I wonder why every time I turn around you're running a new experiment on me. Without my permission, I might add." She released the button on the intercom and rested her head against wall. *If the bullet he extracted belonged to the Sig, how did it end up going off inside the backpack?*

"I'm kidding. In all seriousness, I just wanted to make sure you weren't losing your senses."

River moved her head away from the wall as she heard a signal of three beeps coming from the intercom. She pressed the video feed key that began flashing. Xavier appeared on the interface that projected from it. He grabbed a ziplock baggie off his desk and brought it up by his face so River could see it. Inside the baggie was a single bullet.

"The bullet I extracted belonged to an MP5. I noticed the coloring was off and ran some tests. According to my lab results, the bullet was coated with some kind of nasty venom, which may or may not explain why you had such a fast-spreading infection. I'm running a few more tests on your leg and blood to be certain."

"Can I hope for speedy results, or do I have the clear-all from the doctor so I can start my next objective?"

"Depends on your objective. And by the way, my results are always fast. Surgeries are just the one thing I have to take my time on... ya know. Nerves and stuff. Real cutting-edge, black-market technology."

"Do I have the go-ahead or not?" she asked angrily. Xavier had been nothing short of invaluable to River since they'd met. However, there were some days when she just wanted to knock him on his ass. Today was beginning to shape up to one of those days.

"I'll allow it. However, you must stop by the lab before you leave. I didn't get a chance to do the maintenance on your arm because I wanted to make sure the precision on your leg was properly calibrated with the chipset in your brain. I also took the liberty, while you were sleeping, to properly control the weight distribution ratio between your prosthetics to avoid you being right-side heavy."

River flexed her arms and shook out her legs in front of her. Once again, her prosthetics felt as natural and normal as her actual limbs. An overwhelming urge to both hug and slap Xavier came to mind.

"Thanks, Xavier," she mumbled before hitting the off key on the intercom.

River rubbed her eyes and sighed heavily as she headed through the doorway. She loved and hated the Axler in equal measure. She loved that it was a safe base of operations and refuge for those getting away from the craziness that was happening out in the world. She hated it for almost the exact same reason. It was never safe to travel for long periods of time aboveground. Not that anyone really tried except for herself and the individuals belonging to the Settler's Camp.

Sundered

River and the members of the Settler's Camp generally worked in cooperation with each other by providing each other information and protection against the SGPs. The SGPs, bombings, continuously generated kill lists, and paranoid and crazed media broadcasts cause enough panic to keep the rest of the populace far below ground where they couldn't be touched.

River started hearing rumors a few years back of an entire city that was built underground and sustained itself by water-generated electricity. She had yet to see it with her own eyes but hoped that the rumors were true. However, she also hoped that the current state of the surface could be solved and the government would be taken down for what it had done. Very few people survived their seemingly mindless slaughter, and because of fear, even fewer wanted to raise arms against them.

River walked into Xavier's lab moments later but stopped suddenly as she entered the doorway. Xavier was bent over a medical gurney in the center of the room, examining a dead body.

"What the hell are you doing?" she asked, alarmed.

"I am preparing to do an autopsy after you leave," he answered, not looking up from the table.

"You're not a coroner."

"I'm not a doctor of any caliber either, but you still expect me to patch you up." He looked up from the table finally to look at River. "What's your point?"

She really didn't have a point, and while Xavier was normally weird by every standard, for some reason, the idea of him performing an autopsy bothered her. For now, she smothered her feelings of disgust and decided to change the subject.

"Never mind. Uh, listen…have you heard from Fish lately?"

"She's the reason I'm doing this autopsy," he answered, looking back down on the table.

"Why?" River asked, coming closer to the table. "This isn't something she normally—oh my god! Is this Leon?"

"I believe she said this was her brother… so yes."

"What happened?"

"Apparently, Fish herself had to put him down. Leon had been acting strange as of late and more recently had gone into some berserker-like state, attacking anything and everything." Xavier picked up a pair of scissors and began snipping off Leon's clothes.

"So she wants you to conduct an autopsy to find out exactly what caused the berserker episode?"

"In a nutshell, yes," Xavier said as he removed the snipped shirt off the dead man's chest, exposing an extremely purple and pulsating mass.

"Whoa. What the hell is that?" River reached out as if to poke the mass. Xavier cut her off halfway.

"That"—he said, turning her around toward his desk—"is the reason this autopsy is going to take a whole hell of a lot more time."

A loud chirping sound began resonating from Xavier's desk. He sighed heavily as he picked up the Tilithe, a small clear triangle-shaped device that was sitting on the edge. The Tilithe functioned similarly to a telephone except that it transmitted hollowed messages along the sound barrier until it reached its targeted *barrier gate*. Barrier gates, in this case, were the other Tilithe triangles that were created alongside it. Xavier was just putting the finishing touches on this particular device when Glorious Fish stopped by earlier with her brother's dead body. After assuring her he would do everything within his skillset to analyze her brother, he handed her one of the triangles before she left.

Xavier flipped the top point of the triangle back, causing a holographic image of Glorious Fish's gorgeous face to appear.

"Hello, Frosty, have you had a chance to perform that autopsy yet?" her smooth and sultry voice projected from the Tilithe with absolute clarity.

"Sorry, Fish, I just got him prepped, but I haven't had a chance to fully examine him yet. Was too busy putting River back together

Sundered

again. She's still here by the way." Xavier handed the Tilithe to River and walked past her to grab his maintenance case.

"Hi, Fish...it's been awhile," River said, staring at the little triangle in her hands.

"River, darling, I haven't heard from you in several months. Are you all right? I was worried you were killed."

"Sorry... there were a few more difficulties to overcome getting back. Not to mention near the tail end of my journey home, I had gotten shot in the leg." She placed the Tilithe down on Xavier's desk and sat down in front of it as Xavier came back with his maintenance case.

"Were you able to find out anything in that mainframe?" Glorious Fish asked, a look of concern crossing over the holographic image of her face.

"Quite a bit actually. After Xavier finishes up with my arm here, I'm gonna head to the Settler's Camp to have a meeting with you." She paused for a moment before adding, "By the way, I'm so sorry about Leon."

"Oh, darling... thank you. I can't quite accept the condolences for his death, even from you. I have a hunch as to what caused his psychosis/berserker state, but I wanted Frosty to check for sure. Who knows? This may very well be our just deserts because of how we choose to live out here."

"I'll let you know once I've concluded my report, Fish. Meanwhile, keep the Tilithe on you so I can let you know as soon as possible or if something else comes up. River will be along soon to see you, don't worry," Xavier hastily closed the connection.

"That was awfully abrupt. In a rush to get rid of me?" River asked, watching Xavier as he used one of his tools to release the brackets, keeping the two halves of her arm together.

"In so many words, yes. I also have a weird suspicion I need to look into."

He checked to make sure all the actuators were still connected before tightening the shield plates above them. "Don't pout. I know you're itching to be out and about again."

He pressed hard on each of the sensor pads located within the fingertips and made sure her eyes flashed with each press to know her chipset was still picking up the signals. Afterward, he brought up the command line interface for the prosthetic and made sure it still reflexed appropriately and that each of the directives for her arm was still functioning properly. Satisfied that everything within the prosthetic was still working as it should, Xavier closed up her arm and retightened the brackets.

"There. All done. Despite how rough of a condition you were in when you arrived, your arm was just fine. Goes to show my inventions aren't cheaply done." He winked at her before closing up the maintenance case and putting it away.

"Is this the official doctor's okay for me to get off medical leave?" River asked as she stood up and stretched out her arms.

"Yep. You're all set. Although, I do have a present to tell you about before you leave. I believe you'll find this to come in handy and hopefully won't be too mad at me for making the decision to amputate your leg without your consent."

"I'll be the judge of that. What's the present?" she asked suspiciously.

"You'll see. Run the sniper directive through your chipset."

River brought her arm up and hesitated before typing in the directive. The word *activated* sprawled across her vision as her leg prosthetic began to peel itself backward and convert itself into a stock for the sniper rifle hidden inside. River gasped loudly and grabbed the sniper rifle before it clattered to the floor.

"So what do you think?" Xavier asked, positively pleased with himself. "I constructed the body of the sniper rifle myself using lightweight titanium. The barrel is based on a bullpup design capable of extending further if needed."

Sundered

River whistled. "This is pretty impressive, Xavier, and by far the coolest thing you've done for me lately." She spun it around in her hands before bringing it back down to the floor.

"Fantastic. And to make matters even simpler for you, all you have to do is turn off the sniper directive and your gun will reconfigure itself back into your prosthetic leg. As an added bonus, all your directives are voice activated too, just in case stealth isn't an option and you need to be fast. Now get out of here. Both of us have work to do." He waved his hands at her as if to shoo her out before walking back over to the medical gurney.

River bit her bottom lip as she turned off the directive and watched her prosthetic leg reassemble itself. *This totally almost makes up for it*, she thought as she covered her mouth. Given that the last few months had been absolute hell, this was the closest thing she felt to happiness in a long time. She left the room without saying another word.

Once he was certain she was safely out of hearing range, Xavier cited a prayer aloud. "May the gift I've bestowed upon her keep her from harm and that she be able to complete her mission today with no hiccups or interruptions. Please, God, keep her safe."

Xavier was unruly, downright crazy, and a bit of a mad scientist, but deep down, he did care for River. He just no longer could afford to put it into words. He did what he could for her, rebuilding her, fixing her up with weaponry, and finding comrades who could assist her in combat. The world, as they knew it, was a constant stream of madness that did not leave room for emotions and feelings to run rampant. That being said, he had no choice but to accept his position of being supportive and prayed frequently that she would make it home every time she left.

9

"Does it hurt, Maddie?" Claire asked.

Madison rolled her eyes. Ever since Jonathon left her with Claire, she had done nothing but hover over her and ask question after question regarding her needs.

"No, I'm comfortable right now. The painkillers were a nice touch, thank you," Madison replied.

"Do you need more blankets?"

"I've got enough. You give me any more, I'm going to roast."

"Did you get enough to eat earlier?"

"Claire, enough!" Madison sat upright. "You're beginning to drive me nuts."

"Sorry," Claire apologized "Jonathon didn't exactly leave the greatest amount of information for me to work with."

"It's all right." Madison lay back down on the couch and closed her eyes. "I normally don't ask for too much. 'Course, I really can't do too much either."

Claire moved the recliner closer to the couch and sat down.

"Hey…are you able to stay up and maybe we can…chat? Catch up, maybe?"

"I suppose." Madison gathered up the blanket she was using to cover herself and sat up. "Although, you're not gonna start mothering over me again, are you?"

Sundered

Claire chuckled. "No, I got the hint. I imagine if you needed anything, you'd let me know."

"Good. So before we begin this…talk, there's a few things we should prepare just in case I have an episode."

"All right. What do you need?"

"Those painkillers you gave me earlier were a tremendous help. If you give a few of those to me every so often, that would be really helpful. I'm not kidding. I haven't felt this comfortable in my own body in years."

"I should be able to handle that. What else?"

"Do you have any medications that have a cough suppressant in it?" Madison asked, trying to suppress the incoming coughs.

"Yeah, lemme go get that for you. One second." Claire rushed out of the room and into the kitchen before returning with the bottle of cough medication a few minutes later.

"Here. Drink this. It should kick in pretty soon," Claire said as she handed Madison a tiny cup filled with the cough syrup. Madison took it and downed it in one gulp, making a face as she handed the cup back to Claire.

"Nasty stuff, huh?" Claire giggled a little as she put the bottle and cup on the table in front of the couch and then handed Madison the glass of water she had on the same table.

"This crap's for the birds," Madison said before taking a large swig from the glass. She began to cough heavily again as her whole body shook with convulsions. *Oh god, they're becoming more and more frequent. Please hurry, Jonathon.*

Unsure of what to do, Claire sat next to her on the couch and began to rub her back. A half-hour passed before Madison was able to get her body and coughing under control.

"You all right? That seemed rather rough," Claire asked, feeling Madison's forehead and cheeks.

"You're mothering again. This is no worse than usual," Madison responded, moving away from her touch.

"Sorry…force of habit," Claire said after some hesitation.

"Did you still want to talk?" Madison asked, snuggling deep under her covers.

"Not necessarily tonight. Tomorrow, perhaps."

"Okay. Well, if you don't mind, I'd like to take this advantage of having my coughing under control to get some proper sleep."

"Sure. There's an extra blanket at the end of the couch if you get cold. Sleep tight, Maddie."

Claire rose off the couch and headed toward her room. She stopped at the doorway to look back at Madison. Madison was in the middle of sprawling out on the couch, trying to find a comfortable position to lie in.

"You holler if you need anything. I'll be leaving my bedroom door open just in case."

"Thanks, Claire. Good night."

"Nighty night, Maddie."

Madison awoke startled. She couldn't breathe, and it felt as if there was a large weight crushing down on her head and chest. She gripped the side of the couch to try to pull herself upright. She failed and fell to the floor with a loud thud.

Claire rushed into the room and spotted Madison. She immediately picked her up off the floor and onto the recliner. Madison began to cough relentlessly as she covered her mouth. A few minutes later, she removed her hand as the coughing died down and noticed the amount of blood that came up. She grimaced before turning it to Claire.

"Goodness gracious, Madison. This is worse than Jonathon had described to me."

Madison breathed heavily before shutting her eyes. The weight-like pressure was gone, but she was starting to ache all over.

Claire looked over Madison's face before going into the kitchen and returning with a glass of water. Madison took the glass, grateful, and slowly started drinking from it. The cool water slid down her throat, granting her near-instant relief.

"Does this happen often?" Claire asked, concerned.

"This? Falling down on the floor in the middle night? Nah, this is just a new trick I'm practicing." Madison downed the rest of her water.

Claire sighed and rubbed her fingers along her temples. *Why oh why does everything have to be responded to with sarcasm?* She swore under her breath and walked into the other room.

Madison had a silent giggle to herself but felt pretty guilty afterward. It was not like Claire had been antagonistic or unfair to her, but for some reason, she really couldn't help herself. *It's not Claire's fault why I'm ill, so why am I so resentful to her? Is it because Jonathon offered to adopt me and not Claire? Why, Claire? Was it because I was sick, and you didn't want to be bothered?* She sat and pondered for a while longer and was about to lie down again when Claire came back to the living room.

"Can we talk?" Claire said as she sat in the chair across the couch, her arms crossed.

"Yes, actually. I need answers." *Confrontation? How bold, Claire.*

"I need answers as well. Would you like to start or shall I?"

"Go ahead."

"All right. Why the sarcastic treatment?"

"I have no idea what you're talking about." She began to cough heavily.

"Sure, you do." Claire narrowed her eyes as she watched Madison continue to cough.

"I really don't. Next question." Her coughing grew harsher.

"You do. Stop trying to dodge the damn question and answer it!"

"Water… can't…stop." Madison fell forward, her tiny body shaking with every cough. *She's angry. I won't be able to keep this up. She wouldn't seriously keep water from me to get me to answer, would she?*

Claire walked into the kitchen and returned with another glass of water. She held it out for Madison to take but stopped halfway through.

Madison face contorted in between her coughs as surprise overtook her. *Holy crap, she really would. She's got resentment all of her own she's holding onto.*

"Okay…help…and I'll tell you." Blood was coming up again.

Claire set the glass down and helped her up off the floor. Madison's body still shook as she struggled to get her coughing under control. Pains in her chest were getting more severe, and her throat felt as if it was set on fire. Her coughing slowed, and she clutched her head as dizziness began to set in. Everything was spinning, and she thought for a moment that she was going to pass out. That was until she felt a tiny prick in her arm, and nausea washed over her. She shut her eyes.

"Madison! How do you feel?" a male voice asked.

Madison opened her eyes slowly and raised her head to the direction of the voice. Brad was standing there, a half-empty syringe in his hand. Madison continued to stare as her vision blurred and then sharpened, as if it was being calibrated.

"She's not coughing anymore," Claire spoke up.

"She could have been faking it before."

"If you thought she was faking, why would you give her a shot of the nanomachines?"

Nanomachines? What the hell is going on?

"Madison. Yoohoo, how you feeling?" Brad asked again, shining a flashlight in her eyes.

Madison felt along her stomach. *No nausea. No nausea? Wait, I'm not coughing either.* "I feel fantastic," Madison responded, shocked.

"Good. Try standing up."

Madison hesitated a second before pushing off the couch. It was effortless. Excitement began to build up inside her. "Oh my god. What did you give me?"

Sundered

"A diluted shot of nanomachines. It's just enough to give your immune system a boost and like a buff of sorts to your body," Claire responded from behind her.

"This is fantastic. I haven't felt this… normal since I was a kid."

"Good, you may want to take it easy for a while until your body gets used to the nanomachines," Brad spoke up this time.

"Why?" Madison asked suspiciously.

"It's a lot to explain, but to put it simply… eh…you're running off a battery now."

"A battery? Are you saying I have some kind of current going through my body?"

"Well, the human body itself has a type of a current, but that's not what I'm saying. The nanomachines in your body need to have a charge in order for them to work. You have a charge right now, but periodically, you'll need to recharge in order to keep them going."

"How often will I need to recharge?" A look of worry set in on Madison's face.

"Every three days. Although, I want you to keep this in mind. This is just a temporary solution. The nanomachines I was able to inject you with is a very small amount. They won't last forever. But they will last until Jonathon is able to come back with the medication, if not longer." Brad stepped forward and put his hands on her shoulders to give them a squeeze. Madison returned the gesture by hugging Brad around the middle tightly.

"Thank you, Brad…even if it's only temporary."

"You're welcome." He removed himself from the hug and left the house.

"Where's he going?"

"Not far. We have a small medical lab nearby."

"Is that where the nanomachines came from?"

"Yes, it's where we've been experimenting. It's a cooperative effort between Brad, Xavier, and myself.

"Xavier?"

"Yeah. He's hard to put a label on. I guess the most fitting would be *mad scientist*, but he's more of a jack of all trades in the science department."

"Sounds helpful...and frightening."

"That's quite the app description." Claire chuckled.

"Why'd you guys use it on me?" Madison asked as she began to run her fingers up and down her arm nervously.

"Just didn't want to see you miserable. I can't imagine what it must be like or how you managed to handle it the past decade or so, but I do know I wanted to help in whatever small way I could," Claire said as she raised a hand to lift up Madison's chin.

"I'm sorry for before."

"It's all right. Now can we talk?"

"Definitely. You've got some serious explaining to do."

10

Be patient, River. You can't afford to get ahead of yourself. She breathed in through her nose and slowly let the air escape out of her mouth. It wouldn't be long before she reached the caravan, but she still needed to be cautious. The SGPs were notorious for following around the Settler's Camp, and wherever they were, a firefight was quick to follow. Sure enough, as the wind continued to pick up in the valley, the stench of burnt gunpowder became obvious to River. The most recent battle that was taking place was dangerously close by, and River knew if she lingered, it would be nothing but trouble for her.

She inched her way along the valley wall stealthily and listened carefully for sounds that would reveal the location of the unseen SGPs. Nothing stood out. As a matter of fact, it was too quiet. *This could be a problem. Or it might not be anything at all. Let's see if I can get a better vantage point.* River stepped away from the valley wall to see if it was possible to see anything above it. A jagged rock formation protruding from the top of the valley blocked her view. *Damn. Well, the valley is the midway point between the Axler and the current location of the caravan. I should be safe in the valley for now as long as none of the SGPs jump in here. Should I risk running it? No, if they are close, then that would make too much noise.* She approached the wall again and bent down, waiting patiently to see if anything could be heard. Several minutes passed and still nothing. *Odd. Maybe I misread the situation because I thought I smelled gunpowder?* She stood up and started walking down the valley again.

As she approached the end of the valley, she noticed two SGPs off in the distance. Dropping down to one knee within the shadows of the valley wall, she grabbed her binoculars to get a better look. The SGPs' backs were turned to her, their attentions focused on what was before them. Looking past them, she saw the Settler's Camp caravan. While there were plenty of people moving about within the caravan, none of them seemed aware of the two lone SGPs standing off in the distance. Looking back at the SGPs, she noticed one of them had raised something to its mouth. Zooming in, she realized it was a radio. Not being able to hear what it was saying, she could only imagine that it was radioing in either a request for reinforcements or letting its superiors know where the current location of the Settler's Camp was.

Setting down her backpack, River pulled out EMP grenades and two magazine clips for her Sig. Stuffing the magazine clips in her back pockets, she put the backpack back on and picked up the EMP grenade. Using the binoculars again, she looked back at the SGPs. The one with the radio was still talking to whomever. *Let's see if I can have some fun with these guys.* Holding the EMP grenade with one hand, she used the other to prime it. *Here, battabatta.* Using most of the strength in her right arm, she threw the grenade long and hard toward the SGPs. The EMP hit the backside of the other SGP's head before falling to the floor. Alarmed, both of them pointed their MP5s at the grenade before common sense told them they should run.

The EMP went off with a high-pitched echo, and both SGPs instantly froze in place. Loading the sniper directive within her chipset, she grabbed her leg as it shifted itself into a sniper rifle. Dropping down into the prone position, she used the scope to line up the barrel of the rifle with the first SGP's head. Breathing

Sundered

out, she held the rifle steady as she pulled the trigger. The first SGP fell instantly to the ground, the back half of its skull blown out. *Damn. That did some damage.* River loaded another bullet into the chamber and realigned the barrel to the other SGP's head. She briefly saw the SGP's eyes dart around on his face before she squeezed off another round. He too fell to the floor, pieces of his skull all over it.

Double-checking to make sure no more was around at present, River reattached her leg and stood back upright. The important part about surviving the SGPs was to always be prepared. They had the manpower and numbers to take out a whole city in just under a few minutes. While the Settler's Camp had been able to fight off every battalion or squadron that had ever happened upon them, the SGPs were becoming trickier and were always looking for ways to ambush them. Even though River had intercepted a radio call, she didn't want to take any chances with what they could be planning next and wanted to warn Glorious Fish and her crew.

As she made it to the entrance of the caravan, it was Glorious Fish herself who greeted her. Everyone who had ever met Glorious Fish knew she was quite the character. No one knew her real name either; at least those who did had long since passed away. Measuring about 5'9" with her boots on, she had long blonde hair she kept maintained in a French braid. Her eyes, the color of mud, were said to sparkle anytime trouble arose. Despite being considered beautiful by normal standards, it was her charm by which everyone remembered her. She wasn't shy either, and if you weren't careful, she would literally slip you out of your clothes.

"River! It's about time you showed up."
"Sorry, Fish."
"My god! What happened to your leg?"
"SGPs are getting smarter with trying to track down their victims. According to Xavier's analysis, they're now coating their bullets in some nasty stuff."

"Come to warn us of that then?"

"That and I intercepted two SGPs that were positioned just outside the caravan over by the mountain valley. One of them was radioing."

"Charming. No matter, I'll have my hunters up and ready to go in a few minutes."

"I know I told you before, but I'm so sorry about Leon." River put a hand on Glorious Fish's shoulder.

"My dear, with as long as we've been at this chess game with the SGPs, you should know the queen can't afford to be controlled by her emotions in the middle of a match."

"Indeed, but still."

"This is unbecoming of you. I'm liable to punch you if you don't stop trying to sympathize. A woman must have her dignity, River." She flashed a grin. "Now come, there's a man here who's been looking for you. Dare I say, handsome too."

"What?" River looked at her, confused.

"Don't lollygag, come, come. I'll bring you to him, and then I need to ready my hunters. Of course, once this upcoming battle is over, perhaps I'll finally give him a bit of my time."

"Wait, wait. Let me get this straight. You haven't talked to him and yet you want me to? And somehow, you just know he's been looking for me?" River asked, puzzled as she followed after Glorious Fish.

"My eyes do more than just sparkle, my dear River. I saw him running around the caravan asking everyone if they knew or had heard of you. Apparently, he's on the hunt for some hard-to-find resource, and he believes you can help him locate it."

"Did you happen to hear his name then?"

"I did not. However, I'm not entirely without information. He positively reeked of cinnamon menthol."

River stopped Glorious Fish after her last sentence.

"You got close enough to him to know what he stinks of but still didn't say anything to him? Real classy, Fish."

Sundered

"I aim to please. As a lady should." Glorious Fish smirked before winking at her.

"Whatever." River rolled her eyes. "Go alert your hunters. I now know who's been looking for me." She pointed at Jonathon who was standing outside of Glorious Fish's tent, puffing away on a cigarette.

"Cheers, darling. Do be gentle. I have a feeling he could be some fun for me."

River rolled her eyes at Glorious Fish again before shaking her head. Glorious Fish shook her finger back at her before heading off to amass the hunters. River breathed in heavily and let the air out slowly before she headed over to Jonathon.

Jonathon had just finished his last cigarette and was crushing the butt of it under his heel. He was shifting his gaze around the caravan again when he saw a woman approaching him. Several things about her were weird. *Her hair sticks out like a sore thumb. Who dyes their hair blue in this day and age? And…is that a metallic arm? What the hell is she wearing? Some kind of cyber-suit getup?* Several thoughts swarmed through his mind as he continued to stare. There was something about her that seemed familiar to him, but he couldn't quite put his finger on it. It wasn't until she was right in front of him that he realized who it was.

River Rutherford, the woman he had been searching for, was a shock to his eyes. She stood around 5"6' tall, the bodysuit she wore leaving little to the imagination. It clung to her in a way that made her appear willowy yet sturdy. River was an odd assortment of feminine features combined with metal. Had she been wearing normal clothes, you wouldn't have even noticed her metal arm or leg. Her ice-blue eyes, blunt haircut, and high cheekbones gave her face an appearance of a pixie while the rest of her stature, such as her right arm and leg, projected her as a battle-hardened fighter.

"Jonathon, it's been quite some time since I seen you last." River extended her metallic hand out to him, doing her best to smile.

"Indeed, it has. Not to sound rude, but I almost didn't recognize you. What did you do to your hair?" Jonathon said as he returned the handshake.

He couldn't help but stare at her hair despite how short it was. Last time he had seen her, she had long, waist-length red hair that you could pick out of a crowd. She used to have such pride in her hair to the point where she would gloat to anyone who'd listen about how natural it was. For her to have cut it so dramatically short and dye it on top of that spoke volumes about her.

"I understand you've been looking for me. How can I be of assistance?" She ignored the hair question entirely.

Must be a sore spot for her. Probably should leave it alone for now.

"Yes. Do you remember my youngest sister, Madison?"

"I briefly remember someone named Madison." River tilted her head, trying to think. "Was she the one that was sick all the time?" Jonathon nodded. "What about her?"

"Well, most recently, I've run out of medication for her condition. Would you happen to know anyone or have a source on where to get something that can treat the immune system?"

"Hard to say without having a doctor examine her. What exactly is wrong with her?"

"Not sure, to be honest. She was diagnosed just before the eradication started with an unidentified autoimmune disease. They prescribed her vitamin supplements and something called Cibraline. Suppose to be an immunosuppression."

"Cibraline…never heard of it." She stared at Jonathon. "And you say you've been giving it to her for the past ten years? How is that possible?"

"For a while, I was able to get it from the pharmacy in three-month intervals. That was until the government kill lists started targeting them. It was almost impossible to get it afterward due to

Sundered

the panic that followed. A few months later, a few friends of mine and myself mustered up the courage to infiltrate the abandoned pharmaceutical company that manufactured Cibraline and stole a large stash of it. A bomb fell on that building a week later. That was a little over seven years ago."

"Some of those pills had to have expired before you were able to give them to her."

Jonathon nodded. "They did. However, I continued to give them to her. They seemed to still help, and up until two years ago, there were no side effects." He sighed. "Madison said the side effects were worth it. What was I supposed to do?"

Suddenly, a low-pitched frequency began to emit through the Settler's Camp. Jonathon looked around startled and unsure of where the noise was coming from.

"It's the low-frequency, air-raid siren. It means the SGPs are advancing toward our location, and we need to prepare ourselves." River pulled her Sig out of her holster and checked the magazine to make sure it was fully loaded. "It goes without saying, Jonathon, that this conversation is going on hold while we deal with this upcoming disaster." Satisfied with the magazine, she slid it back in. "Can you shoot?"

Jonathon nodded. "I'll warn you, it's definitely been awhile though."

River chuckled. "Tell you what, if you can manage to not kill anyone from the Settler's Camp or yourself during this battle, then I'll lead you to someone who can help your sister."

"And how, pray tell, am I supposed to protect myself?" he asked as he looked around for a weapon.

River hesitated for a moment before she handed her Sig to Jonathon.

"Take my Sig and these." She pulled out the two magazine clips she had in her back pockets. "Avoid standing out in the open, and whenever possible, aim for their heads. They go down faster that way."

"Got it." Jonathon pocketed the magazine clips and gripped the Sig tightly in his left hand. He wasn't lying to her when he said it had been awhile. As a matter of fact it, had been five years since he had fired a gun last. *Hope I don't miss.*
"Ready?" she asked, eying him up and down.
"As ready as I can be, I guess." He swallowed hard.
River waved at him to follow her as she ran off to join the group of hunters gathered at the front side of the caravan. He followed suit immediately afterward, not wanting to be left behind. Glorious Fish was at the head of the group, giving an eloquent pep talk as only she could do.
"Ladies and gentlemen, it seems our lovely friends employed by the government have found us again. The ridiculous strides that they go through to hunt us down is completely mindboggling. Nevertheless, we must do our part to protect our freedom and to show our rivals the ever-so-pleasant Security Grafted Personnel that the Settler's Camp isn't to be trifled with. Lay unto them capital punishment and let the last thing those moronic meat puppets see be the flashes from our muzzles and our pride of being outside their control. Godspeed and make your mothers proud!"
Cheers came from all the members of the Settler's Camp before separating and assuming their battle positions. Those who didn't fight the frontlines secluded themselves inside "trapdoor" areas hidden within each of the tents. They took with them the essential resources and supplies the caravan needed to survive to avoid the SGPs trying to destroy them. To date, the SGPs still didn't know about the trapdoors, something that Glorious Fish and everyone within the caravan were very proud of.
River saluted to Glorious Fish before making a mad dash to the back of the caravan where the mountain ridges were located. She climbed up until she found a somewhat flat area and proceeded to set herself into a prone position with her sniper rifle. River was high enough off the ground that she could see the

entire plains and valley before her, but not too high where she couldn't differentiate between the hunters and SGPs.

She moved her scope around the caravan, making sure everyone was in position. Jonathon apparently had found himself a spot next to Glorious Fish, who, for today's battle plans, pulled out the long-barrel Gatling gun and had it mounted to a six-wheeled quad. River shook her head at the ridiculousness of it. *Everything's gotta be a show with that woman.*

The first wave of SGPs showed up not even minutes later, their MP5 muzzles flashing everywhere as they began to shoot in the direction of the caravan. River slowed down her breathing and lined up her first shot. Following an SGP's head as he continued to run across the plain, she pulled the trigger and watched him crumple to the ground. Several others went down around him as Glorious Fish opened fire with the Gatling gun.

As River lined up for her next shot, the Tilithe in her vest pocket began to chirp loudly. In a panic, she whipped it out of the pocket and flipped the top of the triangle back.

"Now's not a good time," she said, lining up her shot again.

"It's always a good time. My dear River, you really need to take in the moment."

"Dammit, Fish, what the hell do you want?" River asked as she squeezed the trigger and took out another SGP.

"Nothing but your bittersweet smile. Do try and keep up, darling. We have reputations to protect." Glorious Fish cut the connection.

That woman is absolutely ridiculous. River shook her head. *The sooner this tide is turned, the better it'll be. All right, Fish, get ready. You're about to see sniping like you've never seen before.*

11

"My name is Xavier Frost. I have a masters in theoretical engineering with an emphasis on human construction. The date is July 4, 2197…wait, that's not right. The date is July 6, 2197. I apologize to whoever finds this recording. When you live in hell and do your best to survive the nightmare known as the government, you tend to forget what day it is. Moving forward, I am creating this recording to document my first autopsy in hopes of providing answers to one of the phenomena happening on the surface."

Xavier paused the recording device for a moment. Normally, when it came to trying something new, he was all over it. Even the idea of performing the autopsy was exciting to Xavier, but there was something about Leon's body that was bothering him. It brought a cold chill down his spine, causing all the little hairs on his neck to stand up on end.

After hesitating a moment longer, he decided it would be a good idea to not only record his notes, but to also have a video record of the autopsy itself. Xavier removed the lens cap from the camera he had on his desk and proceeded to try setting up an appropriate viewing angle of the autopsy table.

"Needs to be closer to capture detail."

Xavier picked up the camera again and, this time, attached it to the end of one of the light fixtures above the autopsy table. He

Sundered

recorded a few frames from its current position, wanting to know if the lights were going to disrupt imaging and see if it was close enough to the subject. Shaking his head, he moved it around the light fixture a few more times before he found the perfect angle.

Ready to continue, Xavier started the recording on the audio device again.

"The subject is Leon Andrews. He was a hunter for the Settler's Camp. For those who'll listen to this recording and are not aware of what the Settler's Camp is, it is a nomadic group that travels on the surface, fighting the SGPs. As I go along with the autopsy, I will do my best to describe the condition of the body and the organs."

Taking the scalpel off the side table, he pointed to the large purple mass on Leon's chest.

"Upon examination of the outside of the body, I have found a total of three large purple masses. There's one on the chest that measures approximately eight-inches wide."

Xavier rotated the body over.

"The other two were found on his back, the first one measuring at oooh…seven-and-a-half wide and the second one at nine even."

He rotated the body back over.

"The reasoning for these masses is unclear. I took a biopsy earlier of each one and am currently running each through my spectrometer. Still waiting on the results, will update once the results come back. As for the condition of the rest of the body, nothing outside of the masses seem out of the norm. Subject seemed to have been in good health before his demise."

Xavier grabbed a penlight off the side table and opened up Leon's eyelids.

"Correction. The eyes have a strange activity to them. The sclera is dark red, as if all the blood vessels in the eye had burst all at once. The subject's pupils are narrow, as if they were still able to process the amount of light in the room."

Xavier moved the penlight back and forth over Leon's eyes.

"The pupils dilate and contract normally as if the subject was still alive. This warrants a further investigation. I should place on the record that the subject was delivered here by his sister. His demise was also met by the hands of his sister. A…let's say, creative woman who goes by the nickname Glorious Fish. She informed me that the subject had gone into a sort of *berserker's rage*, whom she was forced to put down. Upon saying all this, it goes without saying that I have checked to see if the subject was still breathing or not. He is not. He also has no pulse, obviously."

Xavier stopped talking briefly to write a note down for himself.

"Full rigor has also set into the body so it should be obvious that the subject, Leon, has been dead for quite some time. However, why do his eyes still react? Is it possible there's still brain activity despite the fact that the heart has stopped pumping? If so, why is the brain still functioning?"

Xavier moved away from the table just long enough to grab a sonic, high-frequency bone saw and plug it into one of the energy cubes he stored by the table.

"May seem a little unorthodox, but due to the unexplained nature of the eyes, my instincts tell me I should start with the subject's brain before I move on to the rest of the body. Best-case scenario, the condition of the external part of the brain will tell me what caused the subject's psychosis and why it might still be functioning despite the lack of blood flow. Worst-case scenario…well, it'll be a mess, and I'll have to run further analysis on samples of the brain."

Xavier picked up his scalpel and very carefully started cutting from behind his left ear over the crown of his head to a point behind the other ear. Setting aside the saw, Xavier then pulled the dead man's scalp away from his skull, separating it into two sections, pulling the front flap over Leon's face and the back flap down to his neck.

"Just pulled the scalp away from the subject's skull. The skull has various tiny pinholes located throughout. There's no

Sundered

puncture marks of any kind on the scalp itself, so whatever caused these pinholes would have had to have come from within the brain cavity."

Picking up the bone saw, Xavier started to cut into the skull, starting from the front of the dead man's skull all the way across until it reached the back of the skull before making its way around the other side. Using this method, Xavier had carved the top side of the skull into a cap to be easily removed. Setting the saw aside, he lifted the top of the skull, exposing the brain.

"The dura mater has the same pinhole puncturing throughout it, just as the top side of the skull did. There also appears to be black flecking along the surface of the mater. I shall take a sampling of the black flecking and analyze it in the spectrometer after I remove the brain."

Using a pair of forceps, Xavier very carefully picked up some of the flecking and placed it inside a specimen jar. Setting those aside, he picked up his scalpel and made a small incision in the dura mater and then, using the forceps, proceeded to retract it slowly from the brain. The sight that would befall Xavier upon fully removing the dura matter was not something he was prepared for. He dropped the scalpel and forceps in surprise and stared at the top of the brain.

The whole top side of the brain looked like it was vibrating. Or something akin to vibrating. It was completely black, and tiny electrical currents seem to jump from random parts of the skull. Xavier shuffled around his side table before running over to his desk to look for a magnifying scope. Using the scope, he zoomed in to a magnification of 64×. What originally looked like vibration was actually hundreds and hundreds of nanomachines scurrying around, trying to repair damage to the brain.

"Fascinating. Leon Andrews's brain is infested with hundreds and hundreds of nanomachines. I…just…whoa."

The words wouldn't come to him. Xavier was completely surprised and a little shocked at what he found. *How did a hunter within the Settler's Camp, who had no way of being exposed to the last medical advancement society had made, obtain nanomachines? And not just a small sampling of nanomachines, but a large enough conglomerate that he would have had to be receiving them at regular intervals. But where? The camp doesn't have the medical equipment to do any extractions, and none of the SGP bases are anywhere nearby.* Xavier furrowed his brow, the thoughts of what this could mean troubling him.

"I do apologize for the stillness of the air. I was merely taken aback by this recent development. For the sake of making an accurate account, I am reporting that upon magnified inspection of the subject's brain, hundreds and hundreds of nanomachines were found upon it. Furthermore, they are attempting to repair the tissues within the brain to give it functionality. This could explain why the subject's eyes were responding to light earlier. However, this now brings up another question. How did this hunter come into contact with nanomachines in the first place?"

12

"Really? Drag racing?" Madison asked, incredulous.

"Yep. Eight years on the underground circuit, tearing up the asphalt any way I could. I was pretty notorious. 'Course, with notoriety come enemies and traps. Claire Richtor was a legend." Claire stopped for a moment and sighed. "But like all legends, they eventually come to an end."

"What made you stop racing?"

"You mean besides the constant death threats and the various thugs who tried to claim my life every time I wasn't driving?" Claire smiled.

"You can't tell me that's what stopped you." Madison's eyes grew wide. "Don't tell me it's because of Brad you stopped."

Claire chuckled. "No, no. Lord knows he tried though. You know back then, when he and I first met, he and his company installed the lifts around this house. Yeah...he was pretty adamant about it. But I...raced until I crashed."

Claire stared off at the far wall as if she was reliving the memory. She stood up from the couch and turned her back to Madison. "One day I ran into Henderson "Glory" Diggs, and he dared me to a race. I couldn't refuse. We raced from sunrise to sunset. It was the most thrilling and exciting race I've ever been a part of."

Madison opened her mouth as if to say something but instead let out a gasp as Claire unbuttoned her shirt and slowly slid it down her arms, leaving her back completely exposed. Her entire back was covered top to bottom with scars caused by massive third-degree burns. While the doctors were able to repair a good portion of the skin with skin grafts, her back still looked like a battlefield.

"Holy smokes. Claire…"

"Didn't even get to finish the race. Glory didn't even stop to check on me either. I learned later during my first round of surgeries that he himself ended up in a similar accident, but unlike me…he didn't make it." Claire pulled her button-up blouse back up and buttoned it.

"I had no idea. Jon never mentioned any of this to me."

"I doubt he would have. While it's in his nature as a reporter to gather information or to uncover secrets, unless it was necessary to expose something, he seldom did so. I always suspected he knew what I was into, but he never chastised me for it. Perhaps he assumed I wouldn't listen?"

"It's possible. Or maybe he wanted you to tell him for yourself? I've asked about you before, and well, he would only tell me the basics. He said that if I wanted to know more about you, I would have to ask you specifically."

"He was always considerate. Which is good because if he just told you everything, we wouldn't have anything to talk about. Do you want some more water?" Claire was holding the drinking glasses in her hands.

"Yes, please."

Claire went into the kitchen and returned a minute later with the newly refilled glasses. She handed Madison a glass before making her way back to her spot on the couch.

"Thank you. Claire, look, um…I'm so sorry. For my behavior earlier…it's just…I really don't know how to explain it to you." Madison fumbled with her fingers around the drinking glass.

"It's all right. Was it something I said or did? Didn't do, maybe?" Claire crossed her hands on her lap, waiting patiently.

"Umm…it's just…ever since Mom and Dad died, Jonathon has been the one to look after me. Even when he and Deborah divorced…and even when Matthew went missing. He never wavered, never second-guessed himself. Everything he did or does, he never questions himself."

"So what's the problem?"

"You just pretty much disappeared after our parents died. It was like you didn't want anything to do with our family. You just left. And yet over the years, you kept in contact with Jon and not once did you choose to speak with me or visit or even inquire how we're doing. And then…and then…" Madison found herself getting angry with Claire as she remembered the drag-race stories she was telling her earlier.

"Maddie…"

"NO! And of all things to learn after all this time you've been gone…that you've been drag racing! Drag racing! Our parents died in a car accident, and yet you decided drag racing was an option. You abandoned your family! You abandoned our parents. You abandoned Jon…you abandoned me."

"Madison…please." Claire scooted closer to her on the couch in an effort to try to wrangle her into a hug.

"Don't touch me. You not only drag raced, but you crashed… and crashed horrifically. And then you hooked up with Brad! For fifteen years! You guys were together before the eradication started, and yet you visited how many times, Claire? How many times?"

"Maddie."

"How many times, Claire!" Madison pointed her finger at Claire.

"Not very often…"

"How. Many. Times. Claire?"

"Four times."

"Not sure what's worse, the fact that you know you didn't visit often or the fact that you know exactly how many times you've come out to see us." Madison contemplated running out of the house, but she didn't know where she could run to. She settled for moving to the La-Z-Boy across the couch.

Claire sat and thought on the couch for a while. She wanted to tell Madison, but she wasn't certain she would understand. Their parents' death had affected her just as much as it did Jonathon and Madison, but she didn't handle it nearly as well as Jonathon had, and Madison was too little to realize what exactly was going on. *There's no good reason to keep it from her…I should just let her know.*

"Maddie, if I tell you…will you promise to listen to everything I say before passing further judgment on me?" Claire asked after clearing her throat.

"Depends. Is what you're going to tell me explain why you didn't visit?"

"It should explain…a lot."

"So spill it." Madison stared intently.

"Well…do you want to take a walk with me outside first?" Claire asked nervously, fiddling with her necklace.

"So we can dodge SGPs and possible bomb drops? Sure, I love nothing more than to find new ways of fearing for my life."

"Stop! Enough. I don't know what caused your hostility to me, but I'm trying to connect with you, okay? And whether or not you believe it or even care to admit to it, everyone has done things that they regret. I'm sorry you think I'm a horrible person for not visiting. I couldn't do it. I wanted to visit, but I couldn't. After Mom and Dad died, I just shut down. Nothing I seemed to do made me happy. I tried everything. Even drugs. I just felt so guilty, and after a while, I started looking for more dangerous ventures. So yes, I got into drag racing."

"That car accident wasn't your fault, Claire, so why do you feel so guilty about it?" Madison crossed her arms.

Sundered

"Because the last conversation I had with both our parents, I had told them I hated them. We had gotten into some stupid argument, about which I wouldn't even be able to tell you anymore, and I told them I hated them. It wasn't even true…I was just being stubborn. I didn't even get a chance to apologize later that day because that's when they got into the accident."

Madison said nothing as she watched Claire try to hold back her tears. She continued to watch and say nothing as she drank from her glass.

"So I numbed the pain. Every day that I had gotten behind the wheel honestly felt like my last. But with each day that passed, I was proven wrong. Every race I was in felt like some kind of crude form of redemption. Like I had to race to give my life validation. Then one day, when I got into my car, I felt this overwhelming excitement. Every miserable thought I had before vanished, and I was filled with anticipation and an unquenchable thirst for speed. For a brief moment in my life, I felt no guilt, no despair. Just happiness and glee."

Claire's eyes lit up as she continued to speak about her numerous race exploits and the number of opponents she bested. Madison couldn't put her finger on it, but she sensed there was something odd about how she was recollecting the story. As Claire was finishing up her tale of racing Holland Stirling, she suddenly fell silent. It hit Madison then that despite what Claire was trying to tell her otherwise, she still felt extremely guilty. There was something she still wasn't telling her. *I wonder if she's told Jonathon of all this? Although if she did, how come he never told me anything? Is it possible he kept things from me purposely? What else is she hiding?*

"I also have a daughter out there somewhere…if she survived the eradication, I mean."

"What?" Madison had zoned out and was absorbed in her own thoughts.

"Before I started dating Brad, I had a temporary fling with Holland. It wasn't until we went our separate ways that I realized I was pregnant. I ended giving her up…because I didn't want to give up racing."

"You really aren't winning any brownie points with me, Claire. Seriously, how much more selfish can you possibly get?" Madison threw up her hands, disgusted with her.

"I was young. I really didn't know any better," Claire protested.

"That's not an excuse, and you know it. How is it that Jonathon was able to rise to the challenge, but you couldn't?"

Claire opened her mouth to try to protest further but stopped as she knew it was futile.

"I don't have a good excuse. And yes, all right, I was incredibly selfish. It's not like I didn't know what my actions were causing. I just couldn't acknowledge them until it was too late. Matter of fact, it wasn't until I was laid up in the hospital after the car crash that I reflected upon them. There was a woman who was admitted around the same time as me. She was in labor. Unfortunately, she didn't survive. According to the police, her boyfriend had beaten her up quite extensively. The doctors were able to save the baby though. The nursery was located right next to my room. For weeks I heard nothing but the sounds of the machines in my room and those babies crying. Finally, the guilt of abandoning my own child overtook me, and all the choices I made prior hit me like a ton of bricks. It ate away at me for months while I was recovering."

Claire picked up her glass of water and brought it to her lips. Flashbacks of the days she spent in the hospital flashed before her eyes. The babies crying. Surgeries. The undressing and redressing of all her burns. Brad visiting her. The painful numbness on her back. The injections. Brad.

Madison shifted uncomfortably in the recliner, pulling on the sleeves of her sweater. The anger she felt earlier was slowly dissipating. In its place grew pity and disappointment. While

Sundered

Claire seemed composed and normal on the surface, she was literally a shattered mess beneath it. She left guilt rule her life and, in turn, caused herself to feel even guiltier. She was right about one thing. Jonathon had definitely handled the passing of their parents a whole lot better. As a matter of fact, he had handled life in general with a lot more grace and respect than Claire ever did.

"By the way...Maddie. You mentioned that Matthew disappeared. What happened?" Claire asked, her eyes bloodshot from crying. She wiped them hastily, trying desperately to regain her composure.

"He...umm...went missing a few years back. It was just after his seventeenth birthday. Jonathon and Matthew had been discussing what to eat when Matthew suggested fish since there was a lake nearby, and we hadn't had fish in quite a while. I remember him packing up his equipment, setting out soon after. Several hours passed by, and Matthew was nowhere to be found. Jonathon went out to look for him but couldn't find him. He found Matt's fishing equipment by the lake along with the fish he managed to catch. There was no evidence of foul play. No blood. No obvious signs of a struggle. It was like he up and vanished."

13

"RJ, take third point by Kirran over at the front barricade. That area is a little bald, and we still need to establish absolute coverage."

Glorious Fish turned away from RJ and raised her hands to her mouth to help project her voice. "All right, ladies and gentlemen, we managed to survive the first and second waves of meat men the government was able to send after our hides, and while it is a worthy cause of celebration, we can't afford to do—"

Suddenly, a gunshot was heard, and RJ dropped to the floor. Kirran, who was kneeling nearby at the front barricade, got coated with some arterial spray. He began to shake his head as if annoyed. Glorious Fish climbed off her quad and walked over to RJ's body.

"What happened?" she asked, kneeling beside the body.

"Well...I don't know how to tell you this...but he tripped and shot himself," Kirran answered, wiping his face with his sleeve.

"Seriously?" Glorious Fish raised an eyebrow. She placed two fingers on his throat and listened for a pulse. Nothing. Glorious Fish blew out air and rolled RJ's body over. There was a single bullet hole where his heart was.

"I couldn't tell you what he tripped on. I turned around to look at him as he was walking over, and all of a sudden, he was falling down, his gun facing him." Kirran looked around the

Sundered

body. "Looks like he might have tripped over the Gatling gun's ammunition belt."

"What?" Glorious Fish stood up and looked from the belt to the position of RJ's body. "Goodness gracious, I know the boy wasn't the brightest crayon in the box, but I didn't think he was capable of offing himself…accidently. Honestly, how do you even explain this to someone seriously?"

Kirran shrugged. "I don't know, Fish."

"Right…Kirran, we'll bury him later after we're certain the vicinity is clear of any encroaching SGPs." Glorious Fish walked away from RJ's body and back toward her quad.

"In the meantime, we need to stay alert in case there's additional waves," she said, turning her voice toward the rest of the settlement. "Scouts and snipers, you know the drill."

The Tilithe began to chirp in her pocket. Glorious Fish opened the top and placed it on the Gatling shelf. Xavier's face appeared before her.

"Fish, what aren't you telling me?"

"My, my, Frosty, whatever do you mean?"

"You know exactly what I mean. I started the autopsy on Leon and found a startling discovery in his skull."

"I haven't the faintest idea of what you're talking about." Glorious Fish opened her eyes wide, surprised and confused, as she really didn't know what Xavier was alluding to.

"If you really have no clue of what I'm talking about, then we have a much bigger problem."

"I'll travel with River back to the Axler once we're sure the area's clear. Thanks, Xavier."

With that, he nodded to her and then ended the transmission. Glorious Fish pocketed the Tilithe once more and looked up just as River reached her.

"What happened down here? I heard a gunshot, and then the next thing I know, I see someone face down on the ground through my scope."

"RJ shot himself."

"He was suicidal?"

"No, for the lack of a better description, he's the village idiot. Somehow, he managed to lose control of his feet and tripped. It's a blessing he didn't manage to hurt anyone else other than himself."

"Are you saying he tripped and fell on a bullet?" River looked at her, confused.

"That's the nicer way of saying it, yes," Glorious Fish said as she stared off into the distance, scanning the horizon. "Can I assume nothing else is coming our way since you climbed down here?"

"I didn't see anything. Seems we're in the clear for the time being." River looked around her. "By the way, what happened to Jonathon?"

"I have no idea. Last I had seen him, he was next to my quad. What's the story with you two, anyways?" Glorious Fish nudged her and smirked.

"Old acquaintances," River responded before walking away from Glorious Fish.

"HEY! Tsk. No fun, that one." Glorious Fish pursed her lips. She looked over at RJ's body and sighed heavily. *Of all the stupidest ways you could die...poor RJ. We'll get you buried shortly.*

Glorious Fish blew a kiss his way then turned around and traveled across the caravan to her tent.

Jonathon was waiting for her when she arrived. She peeked her head outside her tent and looked around to see if she could find River. She spotted her on the far side talking to Tiny George. Glorious Fish shook her head and clamored inside to her tea table.

"River was looking for you."

"And originally I was looking for her. However, I have a bone to pick with you."

"Can it wait? I haven't had my afternoon tea."

Glorious Fish pulled a plate warmer out from under the table and began to rotate the crank on its side clockwise before placing

Sundered

it on the table. While waiting for it to warm up, she grabbed one of the water jugs in the corner and poured half of it inside a tea kettle.

"What are you doing?" Jonathon asked.

"I told you I haven't had my afternoon tea. So what you see me doing is making said tea."

The plate warmer dinged, letting Glorious Fish know it had reached the desired temperature. She placed the tea kettle on the warmer and sat back down at her tea table.

"Mr. Richtor, if you're going to insist on standing in my tent, at least have the decency to sit down," she said, pulling out a pack of Dusty Picks.

Jonathon threw her a suspicious glance as he watched her light up a cigarette. She batted her brown eyes at him in response.

"What the...? You said the caravan didn't have any cigarettes!"

"The caravan doesn't have cigarettes. I do." She blew a smoke ring in his direction.

Jonathon swore under his breath as he took the seat across Glorious Fish. Glorious Fish pulled two cups and spoons out of the cupboard behind her chair as the tea kettle began to whistle. She balanced the cigarette between her lips as she filled the cups and slid one over to Jonathon, spilling hot water in the process.

"You got a preference on flavor, Mr. Richtor?" She blow another smoke ring in his direction.

"I really don't drink tea."

"You better start. Otherwise, this conversation is finished." She pulled out a small box of loose leaf tea with the words *orange cinnamon* sprawled across the top in loopy cursive. Slamming it down on the table, Glorious Fish made it perfectly clear that she wasn't budging as she continued to stare at him, puffing on her cigarette.

With a steely look thrown back at Glorious Fish, Jonathon opened up the tea box and began to toss the leaves into his cup.

Glorious Fish took one last drag of her cigarette, finishing it, before putting it out on the tray on top of the cupboard.

"Can we talk now?" Jonathon asked as he stirred his tea.

"Don't be so impatient. It's undignified," she responded as she began to stir in her own tea leaves. She brought the cup underneath her nose and slowly took in the orange-cinnamon aroma. *Nothing is more graceful than the delicate art of tea drinking. And of course, the wonderful taste of cinnamon spice.* Glorious Fish smiled to herself as she took a drink.

"All right, Mr. Richtor, I've done you the pleasure of allowing you to partake in my good tea. It's not something that I do on a whim, so don't disrespect me by squandering it."

"Right...uh, Glorious Fish? When I spoke with you earlier, why didn't you just tell me who you were?"

"Why would I? A strange man whom I've never seen before comes waltzing into my domain requesting to speak to me. And on top of that, when he is speaking with me, becomes quite irate over cigarettes. You're just lucky I didn't slap you. Especially even now. Did no one teach you manners? What kind of man sneaks into a woman's tent to ambush her for conversation?"

"Forgive my tone, Ms. Fish, but had we spoken earlier, there wouldn't have been a need for me to wait in your tent to "ambush" you." He continued to stare at her as he took a drink from his teacup. "By the way, as a non-tea drinker, this is pretty delightful."

"Like I said, this is my good tea. It's practically impossible to find any more in this day and age. I won't bore you with the tea specifics seeing as you won't appreciate them."

"You're a gentle lady. Asking you why you ignored me earlier is now moot. Although, the only reason why I was looking for you earlier was to find a lead on River."

"Speaking of which, how do you know River? She's been frequently our exquisite establishment for many years now, and she's never mentioned you." She refilled her cup with water and stirred in more tea leaves.

Sundered

Not wanting to be rude or risk angering her, Jonathon followed suit. "Old acquaintances. She used to supply information to me."

"What kind of information?" Glorious Fish asked as she lit up a cigarette. Jonathon stared longingly at the Dusty Pick box she had placed on the table.

"Oh, take one already and stop drooling." She tossed the pack and lighter at him.

Jonathon eagerly pulled one out and immediately took the lighter to it. He took a long drag from it, savoring the cinnamon menthol in his mouth before responding to her question. "I may not look it anymore, but I used to be a reporter. River was one of my informants. We originally met when I was doing a puff piece on her old man."

Glorious Fish raised an eyebrow at Jonathon as they both took another drag. "Even with being an informant, there's usually a time limit with such things. There's something more to this story. And judging by the looks of that cigarette, you're not going to tell me, are you?"

"It's not very ladylike to pry, Ms. Fish. What's it matter, anyways? It's long gone in the past."

"I have a caravan of fifty-seven individuals…sorry, fifty-six individuals that I look after. You'll excuse me if I inquire past dealings with strangers that pass through."

"I'm not here to interfere with the Settler's Camp if that's what you're worried about."

"I have no way of knowing what your true intentions are, Mr. Richtor."

"Ms. Fish, if you didn't trust me, why did you go through the effort of wasting your good tea on me?" He smiled at her over the top of his cup before finishing it.

"Trust or not, I do enjoy a good conversation and tea sitting. Another cup?"

"No, thank you. I'd like to savor the menthol if you don't mind. Not like I'm going to be able to get my hands on Dusty Picks for a while."

"If you insist. Perhaps, after you spend some time with our establishment, you'll consider opening up to me, hmm?"

"I'll consider it…also, I don't know how you managed it, but I'd like my pants back please."

Glorious Fish smirked as she took another drag of her cigarette.

"Never mind. Just keep them. I'll eventually come back for them." He picked up the pack of Dusty Picks sitting on the tea table and pulled two more cigarettes out before tossing the pack at Glorious Fish. She caught it with little effort, a smirk still evident on her face. Without saying another word, Jonathon left the tent.

Checkmate. Although…is it really a victory? He doesn't seem to remember who I am, she thought. She smoked the remainder of her cigarette down to the filter before putting it out. While it was strange to encounter people on the surface, it was even stranger to encounter people on the surface who still seemed well-adjusted. Glorious Fish contemplated for a while if Jonathon was a spy or what kind of possible objectives he could have. Throughout their entire conversation, he was cool and dignified. It didn't seem like he had anything to hide, but at the same time, he wasn't very forthcoming. He also knew who River was, but to what extent, she didn't know. When Glorious Fish had seen them talking earlier, River seemed surprised to see him but was otherwise unfazed.

Glorious Fish got up from the table and moved the tent flap aside so she could peer around the camp. Everyone in the caravan was going about doing various activities. The hunters were busy checking over their gun supplies, making sure they were cleaned and loaded. The gatherers, or those who didn't participate in the battles with the SGPs, were busy gathering the dead bodies of both parties. She made a mental note for herself to check with Dorian later to learn today's death count.

Sundered

For now, Glorious Fish watched both in amusement and with amazement. The Settler's Camp was a group of individuals who, despite how harsh the world had become, adapted and kept a rational outlook on life. Not to say that they didn't have their differences in opinions or their share of arguments, because they did. When things went more horribly than they already were, the caravan pulled itself together to put things back to normal as much as possible. And that was something Glorious Fish was really proud of.

Over the years, around a hundred or so individuals have happened across the Settler's Camp. Each one suffering in one form or another. Many left, unable to deal with the losses they'd sustained, to wander aimlessly until the SGPs were able to claim their life. Others committed suicide after having to face the SGPs themselves. And then there were the small few who stayed because they wanted to live and be given a fighting chance in this depressing world.

Glorious Fish spotted River and Jonathon across the way, and just like earlier, both looked at ease talking with each other. Various hand gestures, agreeable nods, and there was even an unspoken thread of sorts between them. Everything checked out until Jonathon made a gesture toward River's hair, as if to touch it, and a look of despair plastered all over her face. A smile quickly formed on Glorious Fish's face.

"Acquaintances? I daresay our little River and Mr. Richtor here know each other quite... eloquently."

14

"I want to make this very clear to you, Jonathon. My services to you only extends to helping you find the medicine or possible aid to your sister. Nothing more and nothing less. Now please stop trying to grab my hair," River said as she took another step away from Jonathon.

Jonathon stared at her awhile, carefully eyeing her demeanor. Almost her entire being was different from what he remembered. Her hair was no longer a prized piece to her, her tone quite solemn and direct. Half of her limbs had been replaced with mechanical ones. Her eyes, previously a soft icy color, reflected a harsh shade of blue that did nothing to help Jonathon identify what kind of emotions she must be hiding. River's entire composure toward him was difficult to read, and at the time, he had this gut feeling that told him to back off.

"Fine. What is the price of payment for your service this time?"

"I won't need payment…not that I collect much anymore. I know someone who can concoct something for your sister's maladies. I'm going to be taking you to him. The only problem is he's going to need incentive to do such a thing. He gets bored easily for simple things. Shouldn't be hard for a man of your talents." A slight smile appeared on River's face.

"And yet I can't get you to really talk to me." The unknown sense from before was once again warning him to back off.

Sundered

River's face hardened before responding, "That's because I'm immune to your charms." Her eyes wandered from his face down to his waist before coming back up. "You better go retrieve your pants before too long. Let's just say...Fish has a special talent all of her own."

River turned to walk away before adding, "Be ready to go in three hours." Then she was gone.

Jonathon shook his head and sighed. Something about Glorious Fish seemed awfully familiar to him, and it bothered him. He couldn't place it exactly, but there was something about how she held her conversations and the way it caused subtle changes in her face that made him think of one of his cases. She intentionally toyed with him when he went to talk to her, and he still couldn't figure out how she managed to take his pants off without him even noticing. Glorious Fish was never out of his sight in her tent, and her hands were above or on the table the entire time. However she managed it, she was definitely clever and was not someone to take lightly.

A light drizzle began to sprinkle across the plain and over the caravan. Jonathon looked up to the sky. Dark clouds overhead were forming and swirling into one another. It wouldn't be long before a storm hit. Not wanting to deal with Glorious Fish for a while, Jonathon walked over to his Land Rover and hopped inside.

Back when he used to track down certain individuals to get the nitty-gritty on upcoming stories, Jonathon made a habit of carrying additional clothes with him in his vehicle in the event of emergencies, or if he needed to blend into the environment better. Seeing as he'd been hiding underground for the past decade, there'd been no need to. It was not like changing your clothes was going to fool the SGPs. Once you were on a kill list, it was certain death. They wouldn't stop coming for you until you were dead. That's why people lived underground, out of sight, and why the Settler's Camp moved around a lot. Almost all of his reporter habits had died off, save for his charm, and even still, it wasn't helping him like it did in his prime.

Jonathon pulled the pistol that River lent to him earlier out of his coat pocket and placed it on the dashboard. He pushed in the electric lighter to let it heat up and pulled out the two cigarettes he nabbed from Glorious Fish out of his shirt pocket. The light drizzle outside had turned into a downpour, and Jonathon watched through his rain-spotted windshield the various settlers collecting their belongings and/or children and bringing them into their respective tents. He also watched as River sprinted across the caravan and into Glorious Fish's tent.

A soft click from the electric lighter let Jonathon know that it was ready. He pulled it out without taking his eyes off Glorious Fish's tent and immediately lit his cigarette. The cinnamon menthol enthralled him once more, and he let his eyes roll up into the back of his head. His small moment of ecstasy was short-lived as the sound of the passenger door opening caused him to open his eyes and, without thinking, grab the pistol off the dashboard and point it toward the door.

Glorious Fish was sitting there slightly damp despite the fact that it was absolutely pouring outside with a look of surprise and amusement on her face.

"I dare say, Mr. Richtor, that if you're worried about someone robbing you, your feelings are severely misplaced. If we had any desire whatsoever to do so, we would have done it already and tossed you in one of our hidey holes."

Jonathon tossed the pistol back on the dashboard and scowled. He really wanted to enjoy the cigarette in peace before attempting to talk with her again; however, it seemed like she had a different agenda. As if given the command to relax, Glorious Fish began to slouch and adjusted herself to sit comfortably on the seat before crossing her legs.

"Back for another round of interrogation?" he asked as he stared out the driver door.

"No, my curiosity has been sated for now. I'm here for another reason, which, by the way, I do recall you being much sharper than this. I'm a bit saddened that you don't remember me." She leaned in closer to him, the scent of lotus blossoms catching under his nose.

"Am I supposed to remember you? Up until today, I had never met you." He turned to face her.

Glorious Fish sighed. "Yes, I imagine it would be hard for anyone of my past to remember who I am when I look nothing like I did back then. All right, Mr. Richtor, I'm going to give you a few clues."

Jonathon raised an eyebrow.

"Your first clue: you and I had a common enemy."

Jonathon narrowed his eyes as he racked his brain for possible candidates. There were quite a few during the senatorial elections who came to mind.

"Clue number two: we worked together to try to bring him to justice. It did not go as planned."

Jonathon cocked his head. There were two specific cases that came to mind. However, the lead he had for one case had died in a house fire when he was jailed. The other was a man who went on to be a preacher for his community.

"Your last clue: after having you imprisoned, our enemy attempted to have me killed by burning my family's home."

Jonathon furrowed his brow as he stared hard at her face. Up close, Glorious Fish's facial features were much softer, and her eyes, a lovely shade of brown, appeared to sparkle. An image began to form in his head of a young raven-haired girl. The image slowly turned into a memory. Then the memory fleshed out to the case that caused him to become discredited as a reporter. Jonathon's eyes grew wide, and he let out a gasp.

"Ceresa Andrews?" he said aloud, almost in disbelief.

Glorious Fish breathed out a sigh of relief and nodded.

"Oh my god. You survived. Ceresa…I am so, so sorry." In an impromptu response of discovering who she was finally, he pulled her into a tight hug. "I tried so hard to bring your guys' story out to the media."

"I know you did. There was never a doubt in my mind. I don't blame you. We both knew they would try to spin it on us. I do blame you for forgetting me. What's it been...thirteen years or so?" Glorious Fish smiled and pushed him away.

"You look so much different now...like a lot different... surgery?" Something dawned on Jonathon. "The orange-cinnamon tea. That should have tipped me off. No wonder you didn't want to waste your good tea. It was a family favorite, if I remember correctly."

"Indeed. Look, I have no problem with you knowing who I am and my actual identity. But do not tell anyone here who I am. They have enough reasons to hate the government, and I do not want to be ostracized because of my poor excuse of a father." Glorious Fish grimaced.

"I'll keep it to myself. May I ask why you decided to go by Glorious Fish?"

"After the falling out at the trial and the media massacring your good name, I fell into a life of crime. I stole, deceived, and toyed with various other politicians to get the dirt I needed to destroy his chances of becoming governor. My exploits became legendary, and before I knew it, I was working with others to bring down other dirty officials. I was referred to as the Glorious Phish as in *p-h*. I kept it as a moniker, and eventually, it just became my name. The people here never heard of me as most of them are runaways or refugees from areas unknown, so when I told them I was Glorious Phish, they thought it was like the food. I just decided to go with it."

"And the pants-slash-stealing-clothes bit? Was that a talent you picked up while phishing around?"

Glorious Fish smirked. "Actually, I originally developed it while in college. It just happened to come into use while I was phishing around. You'll forgive me for not wanting to give away all my secrets. I must say, it was mighty bold of you to wander around the caravan without any pants on. Takes a certain kind of man to handle that kind of shame."

Jonathon chuckled. "Considering the various individuals I've had to investigate in the past, this is literally nothing. My father always taught me to never do anything that you don't want to be caught doing."

Glorious Fish nodded and fumbled with another smile. She was trying hard to hide it, but Jonathon caught on before she could.

"What's wrong?" Jonathon asked as he reached a hand out to touch her.

"Don't... I'm fine," Glorious Fish muttered through gritted teeth. "You'll find your pants in the backseat. Hurry up and get back to my tent." Clutching her side with one hand, she hastily left the vehicle and ran back to her tent. Maybe it was the rain messing with his vision, but Jonathon swore he saw her gliding. Whatever she was doing, Jonathon had never seen someone move so fast before.

"That's peculiar..." Ash from his cigarette dropped down onto his lap. Talking so long, he forgot he was smoking it. Tapping it on the ashtray, he took one last drag off it and then put it out. Despite how relieved he was that the sense of familiarity was finally placed, Jonathon was concerned with not only what just aspired, but also a dozen questions or so about Ceresa. *What happened during the time I was incarcerated? Was she the reason why I was released a mere few weeks later? Was she truly the one who was able to bring down Senator Lockwood? What happened to her? Some of her speech patterns are the same, but everything else about her has changed. Did these changes occur before or after the eradication? My god, Ceresa Andrews...*

15

"This is Xavier Frost for experiment one on the deceased Leon Andrews. Due to the unnatural findings that were discovered within the victim's skull cavity, I have concocted an experiment to test out the nanomachines, seeing as they were still active in his brain despite the body having no life."

Xavier stared at the camera he had set up for the trial. A sense of excitement was beginning to tingle all over his body, and he was becoming a little worried that he wouldn't be able to conduct himself professionally as the urge to dismantle Leon's body was beginning to intoxicate him. He loved working with the unknown, and as he continued his investigation of Leon's body, new and unexpected developments kept popping up. This experiment he devised was just a means of distancing himself away from the body so he could get his head back on straight.

Ignoring the dangerous voice in his head, Xavier pressed a button on the terminal in front of him to turn on the camera in the adjacent room. The only thing separating the two rooms was a giant double-sided mirror panel, which not only was the size of a wall, but it could also be slid into its brackets to turn the two rooms into one. Anytime that Xavier could feel his sanity slipping, he used this room to separate himself by either performing an experiment that didn't require him to be up close and personal or

Sundered

locking himself into that room with a lock that disengaged after a set time had elapsed. Today was the former.

Adjusting his glasses, Xavier checked his monitors to make sure the electrodes were properly connected and the electricity line in the adjacent room was ample and stable. Diagnostics determined no problems and gave off a bright-green light. Xavier then turned his attention to the voltage control and began speaking to the camera again.

"The victim is lying on a gurney in the next room with electrodes attached to his head and limbs. The experiment I'm conducting is going to cause electrical pulses to shoot his body. Because I found nanomachines in his head, there is a possibility of there being nanomachines throughout his entire body. I've already got an electrical line established in there, and I'll be firing it at three different settings. After each electrical pulse is fired, I'll be collecting and monitoring the results from my terminal here. I will then repeat the results back to the camera. Let's begin."

Xavier flipped the first switch on the voltage control. A soft hum began to resonate from the machine as it warmed up and then fired its first pulse. His terminal collected no new activity from Leon's body. Xavier waited another minute and carefully checked his monitor. Still no new activity.

"The first electrical pulse was fired at fifty amps. No activity has been established. No changes to the nanomachines in his head."

Xavier turned his attention back to the body as he flipped the second switch. A louder hum could be heard from the machine as it powered up further and fired the second pulse. Almost instantaneously, Leon's body twitched and then flopped onto the floor as if the electrical component that went through it shocked some life into it. Xavier watched as Leon's body pushed itself to its hands and knees, coughing heavily while doing so. Whirring and trill noises could be heard from the terminal as it began to compute the data unfolding before Xavier. Xavier checked over the holographic monitor again, this time flipping the various screens.

"The second electrical pulse was fired at 120 amps. New activity has arisen. Matter of fact, the victim's body, after receiving the second pulse, flopped onto the floor before it managed to push itself to its hands and knees all the while coughing. According to my data readouts, the victim is actually breathing and has a heartbeat of 100/70. Strangely enough, there isn't much activity being registered from the brain. Hang on."

Xavier flipped more screens and spun the dial that appeared. The area in front of him took on a transparent appearance of a 4D holographic scanner.

"Scanning in progress. Please wait," a robotic voice called out from the ceiling.

The corpse of Leon shouted at the sight of the lights flashing around the room and struggled to fit himself under the gurney. Xavier watched with great interest.

"Absolutely fascinating. The body has managed to crawl under the gurney in an attempt to hide itself. Moving forward, I am going to be referring to the victim by a *he* and by his name, seeing as he is currently running around shouting at the walls. Side note, he seems unable to speak intelligibly."

The 4D scan finished and displayed an entire layout of Leon's inner and outer body on the monitor. The flashing lights died out, and the adjacent room went back to normal. Leon cautiously pulled himself out from under the gurney as Xavier stared over his body scans.

"Previously I had documented in the autopsy I attempted earlier that the topside of his skull had several pinholes scattered all over. According to this scan, the pinholes have all disappeared. This tells me that the nanomachines in his head, and possibly throughout his body, are designed for repair. However—and I apologize I just thought of this—if the nanomachines in his body were built for repair, why weren't they able to repair him

Sundered

before? I can confirm the ones in the brain were attempting to do something, but their efforts were in vain because the rest of the body wasn't alive. Can it be assumed that the electrical pulses gave them a kind of supercharge? Was the charge the result of both pulses or just the second one? After the first pulse was fired, my instruments picked up no changes. Hang on."

Xavier reexamined the voltage control. The dial was set to constant. Xavier face-palmed before laughing to himself. "Ladies and gentleman, or whoever may listen to this, I just discovered that before I fired the second pulse, I accidently switched it to constant instead of pulse. So what this means is…I need to turn off the current to see how it affects Leon's body, and whether or not this is a fluke why he's alive…fascinating."

A look of devilish intent appeared on Xavier's face. He rubbed his hands together in anticipation as Leon continued to stare around the room, the electrodes on his chest glistening. Xavier slowly placed his hand over the switch, sweat beading off his face. Leon scoped around the room once more but stopped abruptly as Xavier's eyes met his. With bated breath, Xavier flipped the switch. Leon's body dropped immediately to the floor, and a level of euphoria came over Xavier. Breathing heavily, he stroked his face, wiping away the accumulated sweat. Xavier always wondered what it would be like to have control over someone's life and death. He never imagined in his wildest dreams that he would perform an autopsy, let alone on Leon Andrews. He couldn't have predicted that he would be bringing someone back to life either.

Licking his lips, Xavier flipped the switch on the voltage control again. The machine hummed back to life, firing a beam of concentrated electricity back into the other room. Leon's body shook on the floor, this time, a seizure taking over his body. Xavier let out an exaggerated sigh and flipped the machine off. *I should have known that this was going to be too good to be true.* He fussed to himself awhile before realizing that he had left the recorder on. Turning his attention back to it, he began to speak aloud once more.

"In light of my error earlier, I turned off the voltage to figure out what would happen to Leon. Upon turning off the constant current, Leon dropped immediately to the floor, dead once more. When I turned the machine back on, supplying the electricity back to the body, this time, the victim went into a seizure. I was then forced to turn the machine off once more to avoid causing any other complications. That, and I don't want to explain to Glorious Fish why I had designed and enacted an experiment on her now twice-deceased brother. I have a feeling she'd be less than forthcoming, especially if I revealed some of my intentions in doing so. To conclude this video recording, the experiment on the nanomachines in Leon's body was both informative and a bit disappointing at the same time. For my next experiment, I propose conducting a similar, if not the same reenactment, on an SGP. That's sure to answer a few other questions."

16

"Whoa, whoa, whoa, easy now, Fish." River barely caught Glorious Fish as she came stumbling inside her tent. "What happened? What's wrong?"

"Nothing. Argggh...just help me get to my cot." Glorious Fish's face contorted as pain shot across her chest and stomach again. *Not again...not again. Why now of all times?* She wrapped her arms around her stomach as River laid her gently onto her cot.

"This isn't the first time I've seen you like this." River frowned. "When are you going to be upfront with me about this?"

"Aggg...eeeeh...I was hoping never. Honestly, this isn't the type of thing you want to admit to someone, especially when one's pride is at stake." Glorious Fish closed her eyes to concentrate on her breathing. After a short moment passed, she spoke again. "I'll tell you...but it's going to have to wait for a while. I want to find out Frosty's findings about my brother's body first." She breathed out heavily before continuing, "Which brings me to the next order of business! I'm going with you and Jonathon to the Axler."

"And I'm not supposed to question this beforehand? What the hell, Fish? Don't you trust me by now?" River scoffed and then scowled at her.

"Oh, don't scowl, darling. It'll wrinkle that pretty face of yours." Glorious Fish paused for a moment as she sat upright on the cot. "It's got nothing to do with trusting you...there's just some questions I need answered before I can move on to yours."

"Does Leon's autopsy have something to do with what's going on with you as well?" River raised an eyebrow as she contemplated the possible things Xavier could have found.

"I can see you're not going to let this go. To some degree, yes...and bah bah bah." Glorious Fish saw River was going to speak again and shushed her. "The short version is Leon and I were exposed to something that's had some adverse effect on our bodies. Matter of fact, all of the settlers here had been exposed to it at one point or another. Just leave it at that."

"Fine." River shook her head and turned it as Jonathon came walking through the front flap of the tent.

"So much for leaving in three hours." Jonathon, with pants, strode over to the tea table. "Rainstorms aren't common for this area. However...it doesn't seem to be letting up anytime soon."

"Like you would know what's common for the plains. You're a city boy. City boys don't tend to leave their comfort zones." River got up from Glorious Fish's bedside and came to sit across Jonathon at the table.

"I'm here, aren't I? Regardless of the shitty situations we have happening in all of Sunderi, I'm here. I'm still looking to get the damn Cipraline that my sister, Madison, needs. So if you aren't going to help me get the meds she needs, tell me now so I can start my search elsewhere."

"Keep your pants on. I already told you I would help you." River smothered the urge to smile. Glorious Fish, on the other hand, had a small chuckle to herself in the corner.

"I'll do my best to hold on to my pants. However, in my experience, I've learned that regardless of what you do or watch, your pants can disappear without a moment's notice." He shot a look at River before leaning back on the chair, his arm thrown over the back.

Sundered

Glorious Fish watched from her bedside the awkward glances that Jonathon and River kept shooting at each other. *Not very subtle, are they? Given their lack of niceties for each other, there must be old, old history. Or perhaps lack of history. Although, either option arouses questions why Jonathon was looking for River's help anyways. Does he receive inside information from somewhere about the various activities she conducts around here? Or does he specifically keep tabs on her? He knew she was still alive. This past decade, thousands upon thousands have passed away, and yet he knew without a doubt that River survived somehow. And yet he believed on some level originally that I was killed during the eradication. Is it out of foolishness or some kind of fondness for the past that he chooses to trust her? Not that she's unworthy of trust or anything...but still, there's more to Jonathon than I remember.*

Before she could continue her thought process forward, Tiny George and Kirran busted into her tent, both out of breath and coated in blood. A fresh gash on Kirran's face let her know that he had barely dodged a bullet. Tiny George's left shoulder had been torn to shreds. Evidently, there were SGPs still in the area. Glorious Fish jumped out of bed to stand before them.

"Sit, rep quickly," Glorious Fish said as she eyed Tiny George's shoulder. Several layers of tissue and muscle had been cut very jaggedly, as if a saw had been taken to it.

"There's a hundred SGPs in the plains currently. Our scout reports detail them coming from the valley to the south and from the paved roads to the east. Our frontline also tells of a new unit type among them. This unit has thus far been proven to be quite problematic," Kirran responded, staring directly at Glorious Fish.

"What kind of unit?" She narrowed her eyes on him.

"It's mechanized. We haven't been able to confirm or deny if there's a person inside controlling it or not, but it has some impressive weaponry that makes it quite difficult to get close to it. Out of the hundred SGPs, there seems be about twenty of these within their ranks," Tiny George spoke up this time as he held onto his arm just below the shoulder. As Tiny George was part of the frontline, Glorious Fish could only surmise that the information he had given her was seen from his own eyes.

"If it's mechanized, it's not going to last for very long out here in the rain. What else do we know about this new unit?" River stood up from the table.

"I apologize, ma'am, but it's not a complete report. What we do know is each one of the metal units has two revolving miniguns mounted on their front sides. They are also able to launch miniature spinning saw-blade projectiles from the slots on their 'arms.' They don't seem to move too fast, thanks to the heavily pressurized legs they have. With every step it takes, hot steam blows out backside. The speed at which the minigun fires is quite concerning though. It can also swivel the top part of its body 270 degrees. Thick metal plating covers the unit, but there seems to be a small area on the backside that's exposed. Although I can't fully confirm that it's exposed as I was dodging saw blades." Tiny George looked at the floor. "They came out of nowhere, Fish…we've lost twenty men already just from two of those mechanized units."

"How'd they get so close without us hearing? What happened to our sirens? Shit…we're gonna need to mobilize immediately." Glorious Fish looked at Kirran. "Who do we have left?"

"Our death count has risen to thirty-one, Fish. Injuries were numerous this morning, but many of them were non–life-threatening. Those who were caught in the mechanized unit's sights were immediately killed. Sad to say…our entire frontline is gone. Save for Tiny George here. He lucked out by catching an SGP off guard and using him as a shield. As for the sirens… it seems the SGPs were able to take them out without alerting us by attacking them using the sound of the heavy downpour as cover."

That's awfully clever for SGPs, which means it's not safe here anymore. Our days on the surface are severely limited. I need to move

Sundered

the survivors…and quickly. They won't last very long against these new opponents. Glorious Fish paced around the tent for a moment before talking to River. "River…this is drastic but necessary. There's twenty-five of the settlers left, and with the frontline gone, that means only the gatherers and the children are left. Can we move them all to the Axler? There's no way they'll survive here."

"Twenty-five? Hmm…the Axler should have enough room. Getting there is going to be tough but should be doable. I'll let Xavier know to receive us…maybe he can whip something up in the meantime to help us out," River replied before turning away to contact Xavier.

"Great. I'll round up everyone and see if we can set up groups to keep everyone together. Jonathon? I saw you had a Land Rover. Can we get you to do transport?" Glorious Fish stepped in front of him, staring deeply into his eyes. If he wasn't willing to cooperate to get her people out, she was going to have to take even more drastic measures to steal his vehicle. With their current predicament, this was no time to be selfish. To her relief, he didn't argue.

"You don't even need to ask. As long as someone lets me know where I'm going, I'll get everyone that I can out." Jonathon patted her shoulder.

"Perfect. George, Kirran, and myself will set up a diversion to pull the SGPs attention away from the camp. While they're distracted, River will lead you and all the rest of our people to their underground base, the Axler. We'll follow afterward as soon as we can. You are not, under any circumstances, to come back for us until you're absolutely positive that all of the settlers are safely tucked away. Is that clear?" Glorious Fish looked around the room at everyone. Each one of them nodded in agreement. She smiled in return. "Good, now go. With the rain still ongoing, we can use this to our advantage. Godspeed, and don't go getting yourselves killed."

"All right, Jon, we've got all eight of the children in your Land Rover. We've got the steel horse trailer attached to the back of it. Sixteen of the adults and as much of their personal belongings as we could possibly stuff are in it. The trailer should stand up to bullet fire for a little while if need be…but it won't last if it gets hit by one of those saw blades. I'll be following behind you on one of Fish's quads with the last settler, taking out any SGPs we can." River tapped on the roof of the Land Rover. "Because the SGPs are stationed around the south valley and the areas to the east, we have to take the long way back to the Axler by going west. Now I've already contacted Xavier, and he said he'd be able to provide air support if we can reach the main road that leads to Jackvale. That's six miles away."

"Jackvale…yeah, I know where that's at. But we're heading toward the main road that can take you to it?" Jonathon started up the engine.

"You can't miss it. The road used to have a tollbooth about fifteen years ago. However, before the eradication went full force, they leveled it and stationed six watchtowers in intervals along the road. Whatever you do, do not go to Jackvale. That entire area is under quarantine due to the poison gas clouds that have accumulated in the last thirty years. Just take the main road south until you reach the fourth watchtower then travel east, past the entrance to the valley, until you get to the Antec River.

"Follow the river south and you'll come across an extremely large willow tree. There's a hidden conveyor driveway behind the willow tree. Detach the horse trailer and park the Land Rover and the horse trailer side by side on the driveway. When the interface pops up, tell it to 'initiate emergency protocols.' It's very important you remember this because without the proper wording, it will seal off the Axler, leaving you guys stranded outside. Once you've spoken to it, the driveway will lower into our base, and another one will take its place. Any questions?" River stared at him.

"I always have questions but none that pertain to those directions you've just given me. Visibility is going to be terrible in the area…but I'll be careful. You better do the same, River."

River nodded. Before she could turn away, Jonathon grabbed her arm. "I mean, River…be careful. And I know I never got to say these words to you before…but I'm sorry. I truly am."

River looked at him hesitantly. Jonathon's face was solemn; the past several years had not been kind to him, and his once handsome looks had all but disappeared. His eyes, once a sharp brilliant green, had become a lightless hue of its former glory and had become surrounded by crow's feet. A few scars decorated his cheeks, and the bold colors of his strawberry-blonde hair had dulled considerably, falling flat and thin against his scalp. *What was it that Xavier used to say? Memory is nothing more than a sea of good and bad decisions? A memory certainly is…but of course, so is Jonathon Richtor.*

Jonathon stared straight at River as if waiting for another response.

She shook her head and grabbed the hand that grabbed her arm. "Once everyone is safe and we can take a moment to breathe, we'll talk. Okay? But only when I'm ready. Don't push it. Now get going. The longer we stand around and dawdle, the harder it's going to be to escape. For all of us. And god forbid it, Jonathon Richtor, but if we can't save Glorious Fish, I'm going to be holding you personally responsible."

That said, she let go of his hand and walked away. Without looking back, River could hear the engine and the sloshing of tires against the wet ground roar away from her. She walked over to the remaining quad in the vicinity, where a man she wasn't quite familiar with was waiting for her.

"Are you River?" asked the man.

River couldn't make out too many of his features in the heavy rain, but she could make out a red bandana wrapped around his head. Unlike the hunters who belonged to the Settler's Camp, this man, she guessed, had to be a gatherer, just based on how much smaller his frame was.

"That's me. Who I am riding with today?" River extended a hand out to him.

"Name's Wickler. The rest of pleasantries and conversation bits can wait, lass. Now I was told I was going to be steering while you were shooting, yeah?" She nodded at him. "Good, I hope you don't mind, but I took the liberty of getting a couple of belts so I can leash you to me backside. That way, I don't have to worry about losing you due to the terrain or risk having to circle back just to find you."

"That's actually a good idea. That saves me some worry about having to shoot one-handed."

River pulled the strap of the automatic rifle she was carrying over her head and climbed onto the back of the quad, placing her back to his. Wasting no time, Wickler wrapped and buckled three large belts around his and her abdomen, as quick as lightning. River adjusted the belts to sit somewhat comfortable under her breasts so she couldn't lean over too far, in case of a pothole or other sharp maneuvers. Wickler retightened the buckles, and once he was content with the snugness of the belt restraints, he turned over the ignition of the quad and sped off to catch up with the Land Rover.

17

"Okay, the caravan is officially on the move," Kirran said, looking through his binoculars.

Glorious Fish blew out air as a sign of relief but was careful not to shift her position. Nestled within a small crevice on the mountainside, Glorious Fish had chosen this particular spot because it was difficult to see with slight or great visibility. The overgrown brush and moss that had crept up the mountainside offered excellent coverage; however, it was rather painful. Sharp spires and rough edges surrounded the crevice, and one misstep could literally spell your death.

Split between Kirran, Tiny George, and Glorious Fish, each of whom was positioned close to one another on the mountainside, was a small gun armory. They carried up with them seven RPG launchers, two assault rifles, a sniper rifle, and Glorious Fish's Gatling gun. Glorious Fish also snagged a few EMP grenades from River after they set up the plans to move the citizens of the Settler's Camp.

She informed Glorious Fish that the reason why the SGPs seemed so superior and mindless was due to the nanomachines that they had inside their bodies, and when the SGPs fell within range of an EMP blast, it caused their bodies to lock up and freeze almost mechanically. The effect was only temporary, however, as after a while they went back to normal, none the wiser.

"Remember, River said the EMP grenades only immobilize them for about twenty minutes. So while they're good for a small sweep, there's no way we can use the five we got to clear all hundred of those guys," Glorious Fish said, speaking out to Kirran and Tiny George.

"Got it. We can use them as a last resort for us if they sneak up the mountain. Gives us time to take them out and reposition," Tiny George called back.

"That's a good idea, George. Shall we begin our assault?" Glorious Fish loaded the sniper rifle and cradled it against her body, resting flat in the crevasse.

"Kelco?" Kirran responded.

"Whatever we can manage." She looked through the scope on the rifle.

The distinctive shapes of the SGPs came into clear focus. Moving around, Glorious Fish spotted one of the mechanized units Tiny George had mentioned back at the tent. It was monstrous. Measuring about ten-feet high, the mechanized unit had a combination of humanoid and mechanical features. The details that Tiny George gave were accurate, but it was much worse than Glorious Fish anticipated. To her, it looked like a metal giant outfitted with every means possible to create a one-man army. On the front side of the machine alone, it had two mounted miniguns with long magazine belts hanging beneath it, a flamethrower, a mini-missile launcher, and four arms. One set of arms was omnidirectional and capable of dispensing saw blades through their hands. The other set held massive machine guns of an unknown caliber. Glorious Fish couldn't tell the caliber from where she was hiding. She continued to eye the mech for a while, looking for some kind of weak point. Nothing looked penetrable. *If somebody is piloting that giant, then surely there would be a door or a compartment on it somewhere. Right?*

Sundered

"Boys, those mechs are obviously our biggest problem. Does either of you have any suggestions on how we go about handling them?

18

"I know you're tired of this question, but how are you feeling today?" Brad asked, coming into the living room. *I know I'm tired of asking, but it's critical to note any differences to closely monitor the full effects of nanomachines on the body.*

"I'm good for the most part...although I'm starting to feel kind of run-down...it's been three days since you gave me the shot, and you mentioned before that I would need...regular 'charge-ups.' Is that right?" Madison rubbed her eyes.

"Recharge? Yes. You're definitely within the timeframe for it." Brad came around to stand in front of her. "Can you walk all right? Or do you need me to carry you?"

"No, I can walk." She got up from the couch. "Where's Claire?"

"She's in the lab. Come, we'll get you recharged, and you two can chatter among yourselves again." Brad shook his head as he headed toward the door. *The last few conversations between these two have been so explosive...and mental. That's it, after the recharge, I'm going to take Madison for the surface for a bit and try my hand at talking to her.*

He waited outside for Madison on the driveway lift. She followed him outside not even a few seconds later. Brad approached the interface to the driveway and punched in a handful of commands.

"So where is the lab?" Madison asked, looking around.

Sundered

"Below us. The lab also functions as a powerhouse. We generate our own substance of electricity there. It goes without saying, but we do have a few other experiments we are conducting down there, so please be mindful and not touch anything, no matter how much your curiosity begs you to do otherwise."

"Gee, I'll try my best, Brad, but I can't guarantee anything."

"I'm serious, Madison." Brad looked at her sternly.

Madison held her hands up. "I'm just kidding. Anything else I should be mindful of?"

"Actually, yes. I probably should have mentioned this earlier, but we have another guest who lives with us. Well, technically, he lives in the lab as he keeps an eye on the experiments for me when I'm away. He, unlike you, is polite and dignified. So try not to be a bad influence on him."

"Does Mr. Polite and Dignified have a name, or say I just refer to him as the nameless boy enslaved to you?"

"He's not enslaved. He's here of his own will...'course, I don't know where else he would go at this point." Brad noticed Madison's expression. "He never gave me or Claire his real name, although I suppose it doesn't matter in this day and age. Tempest is what he goes by. Just try not to go off on a tangent on him, all right?"

"Fine. I promise to behave." Madison fell silent afterward.

Brad eyed her as she leaned from one leg to the other. Despite how she claimed to be feeling run-down earlier, she seemed awfully anxious and energized still. *Although I suppose if you've been sick all your life, run-down must feel like a godsend. According to the stories I used to hear from Claire and Jonathon, she's always been fiery. She was exactly that when she and Jonathon arrived, and she's even more so now after she got a dose of nanomachine. Brat-like even. It's not really surprising considering. She is going to have to work out her aggression somehow though. And for god's sake, make her peace with Claire already.*

The driveway lift came to a halt at the lab entrance and locked into place. Brad motioned for Madison to follow him as he headed inside the lab door. Tempest, a refined-looking man of an unknown age, greeted them as they came inside.

"Good evening, Mr. Jamesson. Would you care for a cup of coffee? I just brewed a fresh pot."

"Good evening, Tempest. I would love some, but it'll have to wait until I say hello to my wife first. Can I have you escort my sister-in-law to the recharge room? She's the one we started the nanomachine experiment on." Brad nodded to him before walking off to find Claire.

"I don't believe I've ever had the pleasure of meeting you before, my lady." Tempest smiled before bowing before her. "Tempest is my name. I've been with the Jamessons for the past several years, aiding with their research. Although, I'm afraid most of my duties revolve around keeping the lab clean and fetching the master his coffee. Oh, I hope you'll excuse my manners. We've never had guests…well, outside of Mr. Frost, of course. May I ask your name, fair lady?"

"Eh…Madison. Madison Richtor. You're…a bit much." Madison eyed him as he continued to stand before her.

Tempest was tall, lanky even, standing just over six-feet tall in height. Long dark-brown hair, tied together at his neck, spilled down his back. His face was a combination of boy and man, rugged yet boyish, with angular ears and high cheekbones. His eyes were the color of cool steel, bold yet soft. They stood out against everything else. Dressed in black slacks, a white button-up, and a tailored vest, Tempest looked equal parts a butler and casino dealer.

Compared to the presence she felt whenever she was around Brad or Claire, Tempest was a strange change of pace. There was no cautious demeanor or immediate bias. Tempest projected himself as a gentle yet polite brilliant ray of sunshine. As a matter of fact, he was still standing in front of Madison beaming, waiting for her to take his hand. After much hesitation and several more once-overs, Madison finally took his hand and let him lead her to the recharge room.

"Ms. Richtor—," Tempest began.

"Madison," she cut him off.

"Ms. Madison—"

"Just Madison, please. Don't make this weird."

Tempest's lips quivered as if the very idea of not using titles made him uncomfortable. Madison stopped walking as she saw his face.

"Tempest, you can't be much older than me. Besides, it's not like any lords or ladies exist these days, so there's really no point in knight etiquette."

"There's always a point for proper etiquette, my lady. These days may not be the most pleasant of times, but they're still living times, nonetheless. Manners shouldn't be wasted on just those who are fortunate. Women of all varieties, regardless of stature of birth or monetary lineage, should always be treated with respect." Tempest bowed before her once more.

"Fine, keep your flowery speech, just stop bowing before me… it's starting to make me feel old." Madison blushed.

"If you insist." He turned his head to hide a smile before coughing and turning his attention back to Madison. "Are you hungry by any chance? I imagine the missus is going to be keeping mister busy for a while, and I would hate for you to go without entertainment."

"Can you cook as well as you speak? 'Course, not that I'd know any better. I've lived with my older brother for the past eighteen years…and well, it left much to be desired. Can't fault him for trying though." Madison felt a twinge of sadness as she thought about Jonathon. He's only been gone a week, and yet she missed him. This literally was the most time they'd ever spent apart in the entire time she'd lived with him.

"You're in for a treat, my lady. I won't lie to you and state that I'm the best chef that's ever lived, but I will toot my own horn and tell you I'm definitely excellent." Tempest flashed her another smile before leaning in closer. "I'm excellent in more ways than one." He winked at her before standing upright again and leading her back down the hallway.

Madison felt her cheeks burn as she realized he was flirting with her. She felt her whole face get hot as she remembered he was holding her arm. She squirmed out of his grip and walked faster to get ahead of him.

"Ah, Ms. Madison, wait. Slow down. If I offended you, I apologize. That was not my intention. I meant it more as a jest. A teasing, if you will." He stepped in front of her.

"A jest but…obviously not very innocent." Madison started to feel lightheaded.

"I assure you I had the best of intentions." He furrowed his brow and gave her a sad smile.

"Worry…about that…later…falling over." Madison fell forward onto Tempest as the

lightheadedness changed into full dizziness.

"Hey…Ms. Madison?" Tempest gathered her up in his arms. "Ms. Madison, can you hear me? Goodness…Ms. Madison, hold on, I'm going to carry you to the recharge chamber. Just stay with me."

"I don't…wanna…die…don't let…the darkness…take me." Madison's voice got lower and lower with each word she spoke. "Jonathon…I'm so…so sorry."

"Hey now, stay with me. I'm sure Jonathon nor the Jamessons would want you to give up right now. Just a little longer, we're almost there."

"It hurts…it hurts…make it…stop." Everything was whirling in front of her as Tempest ran faster and faster. She closed her eyes in an effort to fight the nausea she felt in her stomach.

"Ms. Madison? Ms. Madison! Cripes…you'll be okay, Ms. Madison. The recharge room is just ahead." Tempest pulled her closer to him as he sprinted the last remaining distance to the room.

Once inside, Madison opened her eyes briefly to see Tempest set her down into the machine before hitting a handful of buttons on the panel beside it. The last thing she heard before passing out was the whirring of the machine as it came to life.

19

"Wickler, something seem off to you?" River asked, staring off toward the horizon. She didn't doubt that Glorious Fish and her remaining hunters were enacting their half of the plan by distracting the SGPs, but somehow, their escape had unfolded entirely too easily.

"Honestly, everything seems too quiet…even the rain. It's still falling pretty heavily, and yet it

almost seems noise canceling." Wickler didn't take his eyes off the road in front of him. "I did see the back end of the horse trailer for a while, but now, for some reason, it seems to have disappeared."

"Strange. There's nothing around this area big enough to hide them." River frowned as she continued to look at the surrounding area. Nothing was standing out. She pulled out the Tilithe triangle from her pocket to page Xavier but was surprised to find she was already receiving a call.

"River, can you hear me?" Xavier's holographic face appeared.

"Yeah, loud and clear actually." River was a bit surprised that the rain wasn't interfering with the quality of the call.

"Listen, where are you guys? I had a thermal read for the Land Rover about ten minutes, but it suddenly disappeared. Are they with you?"

Sundered

"No…they're not. We were following behind them to cover their escape. Jesus…where'd they go? There's nothing out here to hide in." River strained her brain to think of what could have caused them to disappear. *Did the SGPs manage to capture or take them out when we weren't looking? Impossible… SGPs so far haven't taken any captives. There has to be some kind of explanation.* River sighed. *Please, please don't be dead.*

"Hey, River, I did pick up a few smaller heat signatures. Be on the lookout. Wait…hang on a sec…" His voice faded a bit as he walked away from the Tilithe. River could barely hear what sounded like a radio transmission on the other side. She couldn't make out what was being said, but it caused Xavier to panic. "No way! No no no—shit." His voice got louder as he came back to the Tilithe. "River, there's mines in the area! All over!"

Wickler, upon hearing the word *mine*, stopped the quad immediately.

"No wonder it was easy to leave. They left a trap for all of us." River undid the belts strapping her and Wickler together and got off the quad. It was going to be hard to see anything in the current weather conditions.

"Did you guys stop? I'm only seeing one big heat signature… and it's not moving," Xavier spoke again.

River looked down next to the quad. There was a mine literally four feet from them. If it hadn't been raining, River never would have seen it otherwise.

"Wickler, uh…you stopped just in time." River pointed to it.

"Yeah, literally. There's one right in front of us." Wickler pointed to another mine not three feet in front of them. "I'm gonna go out on a limb and assume that the blond driving the Land Rover hit one of these."

"If he did, there would be a ton of pieces all over the place." *Or we would have felt it at least.*

"It's not like I want them to hit the mines. My son is one of the kids he had with him for Christ's sake." Wickler lowered his head.

"Xavier, are you able to, by any chance, do a thermal scan between us?" River turned her attention back to the Tilithe crystal.

"I can try. Not likely…I may be able to do an infrared scan within the tunnels. Give me a few minutes to make some adjustments so I can scan below the surface." Xavier cut the connection.

"What are you thinking? That they fell below us somehow?" Wickler's eyes widened.

"Can't rule it out. If I remember correctly…there are brick tunnels somewhere in the area. I mean, if they fell below, at least they're safe from the SGPs for the time being. I just hope the tunnels don't collapse."

River climbed back onto the quad as she waited for Xavier to call back. *I really hope they're okay…I know I didn't expect things to go smoothly…but somehow, I wish it did. These kids deserve to have a normal life…and in this current day and age, it's impossible. No matter what, I will fight for these kids. For anyone who has survived so they can have a future where they don't have to worry about the government destroying things left and right or if a bomb is going to be dropped on their neighborhood just because they spent an extra dollar that day.*

River balled her hands into fists as she felt anger take over her. She desperately wanted to scream out of frustration but knew it was wiser not to. No matter where you went or how prepared you thought you were, the SGPs always had a way of destroying any kind of comfort you could build. River shut her eyes as she felt hot tears forming. *Now is not a good time to cry. Get it together, River.*

Before she could move her hand to wipe back her tears, Wickler reached out and touched her shoulder. Without saying a word, he squeezed her hand tight and gave her a nod. Compassion, no matter how small, was always appreciated. River

Sundered

stared at his hand before moving to his face. Up close, she had no problem distinguishing his features. Tanned to the point of being leathery, Wickler was no looker. His nose was rather large and had been broken at least twice. Numerous scars covered his face and through his eyebrows. Strangely enough, his eyes were the same color as his skin. Realizing she had been staring for a while, River swallowed hard before returning the squeeze and nodding.

"Don't let the SGPs see you cry, River. Despite the shitty ambush they left us here and our campsite, we're smarter than they are. You, especially. I've heard some of the exploits. You and the boss lass have caused more damage than this to them. So don't let it get you down, mate." Wickler let go of her hand and nodded again.

The moment couldn't have ended at a better time. The Tilithe crystal began to sound off, letting River know that Xavier was calling back.

"River. Good news. You'll be happy to know I was able to do an infrared scan beneath the surface. You'll also be happy to know your companions are all underground as well...and judging by how slow they're moving...they're all on foot." Xavier's holographic face looked as relieved as River felt.

"Well, that's definitely a relief. Can you tell how far they are from us?" Wickler spoke toward the Tilithe triangle. Judging by the look on his face as he spoke to it, he had no idea how it worked.

"Er...about two miles roughly. You can't miss the hole they fell into...River, who is this?" Xavier peered at Wickler curiously.

"Xavier, this is Wickler, my escort driver. Wickler, this is Xavier Frost...he's an engineer... aw hell, technically, he's a jack of trades. He handles engineering, medical care, autopsies, mechanical surgeries and installation, various experiments... among other things." River rolled her eyes as she said the last part.

"Not that we have time for real introductions at the moment, but it's nice to finally put a face to the name. Fish used to talk about you a lot as well."

"Charming. Let's continue this later then, shall we? I hate to do this to you, River, but I would suggest making it on foot while you're in the middle of the minefield. Before scanning the tunnels, I tried the infrared sensor on the surface. All those mines are antitank…as far as I can tell anyways. So if you travel on foot, you shouldn't set them off in case you accidently step on one. Good luck out there." Xavier cut the transmission again.

River sighed and pocketed the Tilithe triangle before jumping back off the quad. She squatted down near the mine to get a better look at it. From what she could remember from her initial training as a courier, the mine in front of her indeed looked like it was of antitank caliber. River stepped back a few feet and ran the detach directive for her leg before picking it up. Wickler watched her with wide eyes. He knew she had a mechanical arm because it stuck out like a sore thumb. Her leg, on the other hand, was a different story. River hopped in place to turn toward Wickler.

"Better be safe than sorry, I suppose."

"Eh… hold on a second. If you're going to check if it'll explode or not, why not throw one of the boulders in the area? Better to use those instead of your…leg. More weight from the boulder anyhow." Wickler stared at her nervously.

"That's actually a good idea." River's face grew red at her embarrassment. She reattached her leg and walked around carefully to some of the boulders. Eyeing a decently sized one, she lifted it primarily using her right arm and hurled it toward the mines. It landed with a squishy thud on top of the mine, but no detonation occurred.

"Okay, so the quad stays here. Best not to stand around here any longer than necessary."

"Let's go find Jonathon and the kids. We don't know the extent of the injuries. Considering the Land Rover had to have

Sundered

crashed when it went through the ground, and then there's the horse trailer to factor in as well..." River wrapped the strap to the MP5 around herself to hold it in place and to avoid bouncing while running.

"Oh boy. This is going to be hell on foot." Wickler jumped off the quad and grabbed a small bag from the side pouch. Double-checking his boots to make sure they were secured to his feet, Wickler gave a thumbs-up to River to let her know he was ready. Both of them broke out into a run immediately afterward.

I really hope Fish and her boys are holding up, River thought.

20

The Tilithe began chirping in her pocket. Glorious Fish quickly snatched it out of her pocket and set it by her face as she lined up another shot with her sniper rifle. Xavier Frost's face appeared before her.

"Fish. How is everything on your end?"

"I'd show you, but I'd risk having my cover blown. My hunters and I are still partying with the ever so quaint SGPs." Glorious Fish stared down her scope and followed an SGP's head as he continued to walk behind the rest of his squadron.

"As long as you're surviving, then it's okay."

"Can I ask the point of you calling me at this particular moment?" Glorious Fish fired her shot. The SGP instantly crumpled to the ground with a wet splash.

"I wanted to give you an update on the situation over here."

"Oh? Is the rest of the caravan in trouble?" Glorious Fish watched as the other SGPs fanned out, trying to determine where the shot came from. She smiled after hearing the familiar whoosh of a rocket launcher firing.

"Well, first, did the SGPs move their occupancy at all from that area?"

"Surprisingly, no. Considering how much we've been showering them with bullets and rockets, they haven't bunged at all. Something I should be aware of, Frosty dear?"

"Yep. So the reason why they haven't left…is there's no reason to do so. They lined the entire west side of the plains with antitank mines."

"You're kidding. Did Jonathon hit one of the mines?" Panic started to rise in Glorious Fish. *Don't tell me… this was all for nothing?*

"Unfortunately, yes, he did. However, as far as I can tell, everyone is okay still. Some, if not all, are injured, possibly because the Land Rover crashed when it fell into one of the underground brick tunnels. River and…Wicklee? Wicky? Wickler? Anyways, River and the quad driver are right now looking for them on foot."

"This is rather elaborate planning for the SGPs, Frosty. This whole setup, the inclusion of the mechanized units, the Pincer move—and now you're telling me they thought ahead and set a trap for those who were trying to escape? Somebody has to be calling the shots. There's no way the SGPs are capable of this all on their own. They've always acted mindlessly, as if they only have one mission in life and that is to kill people. Not just that…but has anybody noticed that despite how many SGPs we've killed, there always seems to be more that take their place? Frosty dear, where is the government getting so many able-bodied individuals to go to combat for them?" Glorious Fish lined up another shot using the scope on her rifle.

"You're not the only one that's noticed it. I do have an idea on how we could track who was giving the orders, but that requires me to conduct an autopsy on one of the SGP bodies."

"And how, pray tell, would you be able to track them, Frosty? Also…what were the results of Leon's autopsy? You never told me, despite how panicked you were over what you found."

"I can give answers to both of those. Although, you may not like the answer to the latter."

"I killed the man, remember? Outside of molesting his corpse, what harm could you possibly have committed?" Glorious Fish responded without thinking. She almost wanted to face-palm afterward, considering how well she knew the man but decided to give him the benefit of the doubt.

"I assure you I didn't molest his corpse, but I did, however, conduct an experiment of my own design on him. Only reason why I came up with the experiment is because of the nanomachines I found on his brain when I was performing the autopsy. There were a few other startling discoveries as well." Xavier's voice sounded tense.

"You care to explain what kind of discoveries?" Glorious Fish pulled the trigger again, taking out another SGP. The surrounding SGPs started to panic and began firing blindly in all directions. "Ooooh. It appears our lovely SGPs are beginning to get upset. Boys! Time to stand down and stay covered for a bit." Kirran and Tiny George both called out confirmation and settled into their hiding places, essentially concealing themselves.

"I can tell you about everything I discovered plus the experiment I conducted. However, you are knee-deep in enemy territory right now, and it makes me extremely nervous to be even talking to you right now."

"It's all right. We've been playing our cards safe by slowly whittling down their numbers. Let's see. Matter of fact, the SGPs are down forty-six, if I've been counting correctly. Kirran and Tiny George are with me, and they're the best shots the Settler's Camp has ever had. Besides, that last shot I took caused them into a frenzy, so we're lying low for the time being." Glorious Fish readjusted in her prone position.

"Actually, fifty-one, Fish," Tiny George called out. "They just mowed down five of their own when they started firing so blindly."

"Even better. Although, even if we take out all the SGPs, there's still those mechanized units to consider. What is there, twenty of them? We don't have enough manpower or weaponry to take those on." Glorious Fish stared at one of the mech units while she spoke.

Sundered

This one in particular acted strangely compared to the others. It kept staring at the sky as if it was daydreaming and never seemed to notice or care that the SGPs around it were yelling. And now, the mech continued to act oblivious to what was happening around it and stretched its long metal arms to the sky as if longing for a world that was outside its reach.

"Mechanized units?" Xavier's interest was piqued.

"Indeed. Up until today, we've never seen such a unit. Calling them big metal giants would be an understatement. Matter of fact, these lovable tykes have weaponry and tools that would make you cream your pants with envy."

"Color me intrigued, but back to the topic at hand." Xavier gulped. "Regarding your brother's autopsy...well, I only conducted a partial one. That is...on his brain. There were active nanomachines all over Leon's brain, and by *active*, I mean they were still trying to repair unresponsive tissue. I didn't have the slightest clue originally where he could have gotten the nanomachines, but after some testing, I was able to make a few observations. The first being the purple masses I found on his torso."

Glorious Fish cocked an eyebrow. Pushing herself upright against the ceiling of the crevice, she undid her blouse and felt the three purple masses she had along her chest and stomach. Hard and fleshy, Glorious Fish had always wondered what caused them to form and when exactly they started. *Has the good doctor actually found the answer to these?*

"I took a sample of the masses and performed a biopsy. According to my data readouts, the purple masses formed because the body was trying to reject the nanomachines within Leon's body. Before the decade of eradication, the military had delivered the nanomachines as a way to buff up all of our soldiers. Each soldier was injected with nanomachines that were tailored to his or her blood type.

"I was able to decipher a redacted document detailing the experiments with the nanomachines, including a particular trial that involved a woman who was O-negative and was injected with large doses of AB-negative–geared nanomachines. The end result of that trial was a complete mess, as it caused the woman's body to explode under the pressure of the purple masses that covered her entire body. As you can imagine, this was a nightmare for the government, and they sought to completely cover it up. Not surprisingly enough, they continued to authorize the use of the nanomachines, although under very strict guidelines. Or at least they had."

Xavier stopped for a moment to catch his breath before continuing. "In short, your brother managed to get his hands on a few injections of nanomachines that weren't tailored for his blood type. His blood type was O-positive whereas the nanomachines were meant for someone with an A-positive blood."

"That is troubling to say the least, Frosty. This is a problem. If what you're saying is true, then more than half of the Settler's Camp…oh god." Glorious Fish put her hand over her mouth before she said any more. *Oh my god, if the SGPs hadn't ambushed us…then I would have single-handedly gotten the entire caravan killed. As if I didn't already feel guilty enough. Oh Leon, I'm sorry. I'm so, so sorry.*

"Fish? Are you there? Are you okay?" Xavier's voice echoed from the Tilithe. Glorious Fish contemplated closing the Tilithe. *It's not going to do any good to do that. Wouldn't be doing justice to my loyal hunters either. I can trust Xavier with this…if anything, he can fix the damage I've caused at least.*

"Xavier?" Glorious Fish cleared her throat. "I need you to listen very carefully, darling." She sighed. "A long while back, we were moving toward a new location, trying to get away from the SGPs when we realized we didn't have any livestock with us or even remotely nearby. We made due with the vegetables we had and were able to grow, but over time, we realized it wasn't going to be enough. It was a tough decision, considering we had both young and old with us. One day, we ran into a small patrol of

Sundered

SGPs. Taking just Leon and RJ with me, we were able to ambush the little six-man patrol unit."

Xavier listened intently, not daring to interrupt her as she spoke. Glorious Fish paused long enough to light up a cigarette before she resumed talking.

"To avoid leaving dead bodies for the other SGPs to find, we always made an effort to gather up the deceased and burn them to ash. But after not eating properly over a two-week span, those blasted SGPs smelled so good as the flames from the fire were jumping up and licking their bodies. It was like a combination of sweet goodness and pork. As wrong as it is to say, I've never drooled so much over any other food before or since then. And before I knew it, I was eating the roasted SGP. It was so juicy and tender that I lost myself in it. It didn't take much convincing to get Leon or RJ to eat it either. Maybe it's because I was elected to lead our little caravan. Or maybe they just wanted to be told it was okay, even though they knew it wasn't. The Settler's Camp never went hungry again. We set up regular hunting trips called kelco just to specifically hunt SGPs. We told the children that it was lamb meat.

Don't judge me too harshly. We hunted for livestock whenever we could and even kept some with us so we could establish a little ranch. We did our best not to feed the children any of the SGP meat…but you know kids, they love taking food from everyone's plates."

Glorious Fish stopped talking and began puffing heavily on her cigarette. She could hear Xavier breathing on the other end of the line and could sense what she told him caused him to shift uncomfortably for a bit. A silent and awkward moment passed before anyone spoke. It was Tiny George's voice that called out.

"Fish, you're going to want to see this. Remember that mech unit that was acting rather oddly earlier? Take a look at what's happening down there."

Glorious Fish peered through her sniper scope. There was pure chaos unfolding within the SGP circle. The odd mech who was reaching for the sky moments before was lashing out and attacking everyone around it. Blood-curdling screams and the crunching of metal on bone were audibly loud, even up in the mountainside. The hairs on the back of Glorious Fish's neck stood up as she heard more and more gruesome sounds coming from below.

"Oh good god. That mech just ripped two of the SGPs apart simultaneously," Kirran said, trying to keep his voice down.

"Whatever they did to piss him…or her off, they're definitely paying for it now." Glorious Fish watched as the mech continued its rampage on the other mechanized units. For whatever reason, this odd mech was faster and more agile than the others of its kind. She watched as the odd mech ripped off the top halves of each of the other mechs in the area. Inside each unit were two SGPs who were frantically trying to run away from their former comrade. *Well, that explains a few things.*

"It's like the little engine that could—I mean, whoever is in that mech is seriously pissed off. They just literally destroyed the rest of the battalion. The question that stems now is whether or not that little odd duckling of a mech is going to be a problem or nuisance to us," Kirran directed his voice towards Glorious Fish.

"Indeed. You know this would make for a good story later, but instead of referring to that particular mech as odd all the time, what say we give it a nickname?" Glorious Fish centered her scope on the mech in question and zoomed in as far as she could. It was impossible to tell who was driving the mech due to how erratically it was moving. *Considering there's only one target left, maybe we can put these EMP grenades to good use.*

"Boys, I have a crazy and dangerous idea for our little mech here. For the sake of naming purposes—oh, let's call it Mustang—seeing how it's so wild and free. Anyways, as we can all tell, Mustang here just murdered all of its companions and is in a dire need of a nap. Seeing as the other SGPs never figured out we were up here, I believe we should go down to Mustang there and introduce ourselves with a housewarming present, namely these fantastic EMP grenades we have. It goes without saying that this could be ridiculously dangerous, considering how volatile our little friend is, but I'm confident we can handle this." Glorious Fish almost forgot the Tilithe triangle was still active and returned her attention to it. "Xavier...are you there?"

"I am...I'm sorry. I just didn't know what to say. But...it's okay. We can discuss this further later, as I can imagine you probably have masses of your own. Be safe out there, Fish. Don't go dying on us yet." Xavier lingered for a moment longer on the line before cutting the connection.

Glorious Fish pocketed the Tilithe and snapped down her sniper rifle so she could carry it easier.

"Ready, boss?" Kirran's head peeked down into the crevice.

"As much as one can be. Let's do this."

21

How far do these tunnels go? Where do they lead exactly?
Jonathon coughed as he breathed in more of the dust-filled air. *This really isn't good for the children to breathe in.*

He looked behind him at the children and the gatherers of the Settler's Camp. No one got out of the crash unscathed. Thankfully, no one died.

Despite Jonathon's careful driving, one of the Land Rover's back tires managed to run right over one of the antitank mines, causing the back end to fall into the gaping hole left by the explosion. The Land Rover and the horse trailer landed in the middle of a tunnel system and caught fire due to the force of the landing. Jonathon managed to get everyone out of harm's way before the vehicle exploded. Due to the crash, everybody was damaged. Several had broken limbs, and others had gashes. A few of the smaller kids were knocked unconscious and needed to be carried.

Jonathon himself had a gash on his side and an enormous bruise forming on his chest from where
the airbag had erupted against him, cracking a few ribs. With each step he took, his breathing became more and more ragged. The dust and dirt that flowed throughout the tunnels didn't help matters any. Jonathon stopped briefly in an effort to catch his

Sundered

breath. *How far do these tunnels go on? Seriously… none of us are going to last long in these conditions.*

Being underground with no vehicle and no means of communication, Jonathon and the survivors from the Settler's Camp were completely in the dark. It was crucial that they were careful in their traveling, even more so than before. Taking this into account, Jonathon turned around to address the survivors.

"All right, guys, I know we have a ways to go yet…but trying to be speedy while we're all injured isn't very efficient. Let's rest here awhile, and hopefully, River catches on to what happened to us."

Sighs of relief and murmurs from the various survivors were heard. Those who were carrying children laid them down nicely before resting up against the tunnel walls. The others all grouped up within the tunnel reaches and formed a tight-knit circle. Seeing everyone relax, Jonathon stepped away from the group and checked his pockets to see if he had any more cigarettes. *Damn. Must have lost the last few I had with the crash.* He blew out air between his lips. *Oh well, probably better I don't smoke for a while anyways. Between these injuries and all these kids…it wouldn't be very responsible.*

Jonathon felt a tug on his pants' leg and looked down to see a little girl in messy brown braided pigtails standing there. Dirt and blood covered the left side of her round face. She stared up at Jonathon earnestly with her large brown eyes, as if she was patiently waiting for his recognition. He knelt down to the ground slowly as his chest began to ache and coughed. Straining, he leaned on one knee so he could be level with the little girl.

"Hi, there. What's your name, sweetie?" Jonathon asked as he peered closer to her. Upon closer inspection of the girl, Jonathon realized she couldn't be more than four years old. *She's so small…*

"Meena." The little girl brought her hand to her mouth after she spoke.

"Meena…that's a pretty name."

"Uh huh. My mommy gave it to me." Her cheeks turned bright red after speaking.

"She did? Well, I think it was a good choice. Tell me, Meena, is your mommy still with us?" Jonathon looked past her toward the other survivors as he spoke.

"Nuh-uh. I du'n know where she is. I can't find her." She once again stared at him with her big brown eyes.

Jonathon swallowed hard. *If her mother isn't with us...then she's probably dead. But...how do you explain that to a little girl?* Jonathon grabbed Meena's hand. Her hand, so tiny in his, reminded him of the day he told Madison about their parents. An image of Madison's confused face came to mind as he thought of a simple way of telling Meena about the possibility of her mother being dead.

Meena moved her head quizzically as she stared at her hand within Jonathon's. Jonathon opened his mouth to speak but stopped as Meena lightly squeezed his hand.

"She's dead too...isn't she?"

That lump appeared in Jonathon's throat again.

"It's okay. Mommy tawt me about death. She said is not bad. She...she also said...um... is natrall?" Meena stared at her shoes.

"Natural?" Jonathon asked. Meena nodded. "It sounds like your mommy was a very smart lady. She may not be here before us...but make no mistake, she'll always be watching out for you." Jonathon patted her on her head. Meena looked back up at Jonathon. She flashed him a toothy smile before running around his leg to give him a hug. Slightly surprised, Jonathon returned the hug before sending her back to the group.

He took his time getting back up on his feet and thought deeply. *I have no doubt that Glorious Fish did all she could for these people. Neither the adults nor the children have complained at all during this particular ordeal. How are they all so well-adjusted? So vibrant still, despite injuries and a dark situation that's unfolded before us. They haven't questioned anything of what's happened. Why?*

I would certainly like to know why the SGPs have been ruthlessly targeting them. Why their tactics have suddenly advanced. Oh god, I sure hope Madison is well. She seemed pretty rough when I left her with Claire. I hope Brad's not an ass to her as well.

Jonathon sighed heavily and turned around to stare down the tunnel.

"I have no idea where we are and where this leads…but I sure hope River has a clue. Please, God, let River have a clue on where we are."

22

Where am I?

Madison struggled to open her eyelids, but they felt strangely heavy.

What is this? I can't see. Why won't my eyes open?

Male voices.

"Has she gained consciousness yet?"

Is that why I can't open my eyes?

"Strangely enough, it doesn't look like it. Although, there is quite a bit of brain activity. Is it possible she's dreaming?"

If I was dreaming, wouldn't I be able to move?

"It's possible. It's bothering me she's been under this long." Madison could make out the vague sounds of paper rustling. "Everything's optimal. Including her charge level."

Isn't that Brad's voice? And Tempest's? Hello! Why can't anyone hear me!

Panic started to take hold of Madison. She desperately wanted to scream, but she couldn't even feel her lips, let alone the rest of her body. *I'm not paralyzed, am I? Oh please, don't let me be paralyzed.*

"Hang on a second, Mr. Jamesson. Her brainwaves have increased dramatically. It's almost like she's panicked."

"Quick, we need to make sure she doesn't seize. Elevate her head. We're gonna need to check her pupils."

Madison detected a note of concern in his voice. *My god, does he actually care?*

"Should I page Mr. Frost, sir?" Tempest asked in a low voice.

"Probably. Is the Tilithe here in the recharge chamber?"

"Er...no. I think Mrs. Jamesson has it, sir. Shall I fetch her and the triangle?"

Tilithe? Triangle? Claire's here somewhere?

"Quickly," Brad responded.

Madison heard him move closer to her body. With a soft slide of his fingers, he gently moved Madison's right eyelid up. Light poured into her eye, and she could consciously feel her pupil constrict and dilate in response. The sensation was enough to make Madison feel like an alien in her own skin.

"Come on, Madison. You've survived through the hard parts... you just need to wake up now. You're going to make Claire worry. Worse yet, you're going to make me worry."

He released her right eyelid and moved over to the left one. He slowly slid it up and watched Madison's face carefully for any movement. Although he didn't know it, Madison was aware of everything going on around her. She wanted to jump up and tell everyone she was okay, but she couldn't. She felt like a prisoner in her own body.

I'm awake, Brad. I swear I am.

Because her eyelid was still open, Madison's eye focused, and she could clearly make out Brad's face as he stood over her. His face was somber and miserable as he continued to stare at her. He made no effort to hide the tears that began to stream down his face.

Is he...seriously crying? Madison thought in disbelief. Seeing how torn up Brad was about her predicament, Madison felt like she finally understood him for the first time in her life. Brad released her other eyelid, and everything turned back to darkness.

No, no, please. Open my eyes again. Please don't leave me in the dark.

If she had control of her body, Madison would have broke down crying right then and there. Thankfully, Tempest returned to the room with Claire. Madison heard their hurried footsteps as they rushed inside.

"She's still not awake?" Claire called out.

"Not yet. There's something going on though." Judging from the sound of his voice, Madison realized Brad didn't turn around when Claire and Tempest entered. He was still staring at Madison.

"Tempest mentioned you guys monitored a high amount of brain activity. Let me have a look. Tempest, would you get the good doctor on the Tilithe for us in the meantime?" There was a subtle quiver in Claire's voice. She, like Brad and Tempest, was not expecting this kind of predicament.

Everything went quiet for a while. Madison listened anxiously, wondering what was going to happen next. Before long, a chirping sound filled the room.

"Good evening, Mr. Frost." It was Tempest's voice this time.

"Yes, yes…good evening, Tempest. What's happening? Why were you calling so frequently?" Madison had never heard this deep voice before. She could only assume this was the doctor that Tempest had mentioned earlier.

"I'll have the Jamessons explain it to you, sir. It is a rather urgent matter." Tempest's voice grew louder as he came closer to the table. Madison heard a small clang as he set whatever he had in his hands on the table.

"I doubt it's more urgent than the situation I'm already involved with, but we'll find out. Claire, Brad, would either of you like to explain to me what's so damn important?" the deep voice asked, irritation and urgency evident.

"Xavier, I apologize. But I'm afraid this couldn't wait any longer. Do you remember the subject we contacted you about earlier in the week, the one Brad injected with the experimental nanomachines?"

"Yes, how hard is it to remember? There's not too many people around these days for them to be parading around your doors. Matter of fact, I believe Claire stated it was her sister. Yeah, her sister. What about it?"

Madison was a little thrown off with how irritated the man with the deep voice sounded.

"Yes, my sister." It was Claire's voice again. "Her nanomachines are completely charged. Her vitals are optimal. There's well...a large amount of brainwave activity...however, she won't wake up. It's been two days. Did we do something wrong? Did we overlook something?" Her voice turned frantic.

"Let me think... she's not in the recharge station, right?"

"Correct. She's lying on one of the beds we have in the lab," Brad spoke up. Madison wondered what could possibly happen next. *How would this guy know what's wrong? Was he the one who created this kind of technology...er... experiment to begin with?*

"Okay. And you said she had a large amount of brainwave activity? Did you guys bother to check what kind of brainwaves she was having? Because if I had to guess, she's probably projecting beta brainwaves. Do you have a readout on her muscle control, or is there any hint of adrenaline coursing through her currently?"

Madison could hear footsteps scurry about and paper shuffling. *What does adrenaline have to do with this?* A few seconds later, the sound of a fist meeting the table was heard.

"Seriously, she's been under two days, and we failed to take into account her muscle control. Son of a bi—it's not that she's been under this entire time. She has no control over her body because the recharge to her nanomachines rendered the rest of her body to fall in stasis." Brad let out an aggravated sigh. "Xavier, I apologize for bothering you. Because she's still getting acquainted to the nanomachines in her body, we didn't take into account the effect it would have on her normal functions. Christ...Tempest, would you please get 20 ccs of adrenaline please and administer it to Madison's IV." Brad sounded defeated. Madison could only assume that this in itself was a blow to his ego.

"You're going to pump adrenaline into her body to give her jumpstart? Hmm...not a bad idea. Just don't pump her with too much. Otherwise, I think you're liable to blow up her heart. Anyways, if your crisis has been rendered averted, I shall take my leave. Do take some notes of this incident though and keep it as accumulated data in the event something like this happens in the future again."

There was a harsh click followed by silence. Madison could barely make out Claire and Brad whispering to each other before a pair of footsteps interrupted them.

"Ready to administer the adrenaline, Mr. Jamesson," Tempest announced before walking around the bed where Madison lay.

Madison listened with great intent as she waited patiently for Tempest to inject her. Within seconds, she felt the warming sensation of the adrenaline as it was injected into her IV, the effects spreading throughout her body almost immediately. The strange, alienated feeling she felt before flooded over her body again, and she was able to open her eyelids. It was surreal.

Tempest's face was the first thing she saw. His gray eyes were staring down at her, relief filling them as he watched her blink rapidly.

"You gave us quite a scare, Ms. Madison. The Jamessons were going rather crazy trying to figure out what went wrong. Here, let me help you upright." He flashed her a wide smile as he extended a hand before her. Madison hesitated before accepting his offer.

23

"River, look there! There's a trail of smoke," Wickler shouted as he pointed ahead of him. River turned her attention to the direction he was pointing and instantly saw what he was talking about.

"Shit. The Land Rover must have caught fire after crashing at the bottom. Which means they fell hard. Be prepared, they're all bound to be injured at this point…if not dead," River responded in between strides.

Wickler and River had been wandering around the plains for an hour, looking for the area the Land Rover had fallen through. The heavy downpour from before had slowed down considerably, leaving them to have better visibility of their surroundings. The smoke trail, which rose up from the hole caused by the Land Rover, stood out against everything in the vicinity. River knew the SGPs were bound to notice before long and made a mental note to herself to figure out a way to either mask the fire or put it out completely.

River sprinted ahead of Wickler and stopped quickly as she neared the edge of the hole. Kneeling beside it, she peered inside and could make out the charred remains of Jonathon's still burning vehicle and the various odds and ends they had previously placed inside the trailer. But she could not determine if there were any bodies in the vehicle or not. *Xavier did say earlier that they were all moving slowly through the tunnel, so they all would have made it.*

'Course, Xavier doesn't know the number of survivors we're supposed to have either. Whatever, I'll take injured over dead any day.

"The underground tunnels were built five feet below the surface," River said aloud to Wickler as he neared the edge. "If I remember correctly, the tunnels here are approximately twenty-feet deep."

"Sounds like a bit of a drop. Twenty-five is rough on a vehicle. I can only imagine how much rougher it'll be on our legs if we attempt this drop." Wickler whistled as he saw the remains of the Land Rover. "Oh man, that looks harsh. The framework's all bent. I guarantee you there's probably a few of them with broken arms, if not a leg or two."

"The fun part is figuring out how we're going to get down there safely for one, and two, do something to this fire to avoid catching the SGPs' attention. That is, if the damn thing doesn't explode by the time we get into this hole." River eyed her surroundings carefully. *Twenty-five feet is not going to be fun. Wish we had some rope…but that might make it a bit obvious to the SGPs. 'Course, I hope we move fast enough where that's not an issue.*

"All right, so what do you suggest, River?" Wickler was anxiously waiting for instructions.

"Do we both need to go down there? Well…yeah, we kind of do, just because the closest 'entrance' to the tunnels is miles away." River strummed her fingers against her face as she tried to think. *Think, think, we can't risk ourselves getting injured going in after them. There must be something nearby that we can use…ah ha!* Madison pointed in front of her. "Look, the trailer hasn't caught fire. We can jump to that and then jump the rest of the way down. That's about the only real option we've got."

"That's still quite a bit of a drop." Wickler's eyes grew wide as he looked at River bewildered.

"Not as bad. Besides, I can lower you down. Should remove the possibility of getting heavily injured, provided we move fast enough."

Wickler swore under his breath. "All right, let's get this over with. I don't want to leave those kids down there any longer than I have to."

24

"Guys, I know you all aren't very familiar with who I am. But I believe we should get to know each other a little bit. After all, we could use a distraction." Jonathon turned his head as he spoke. He was hoping he could get them motivated enough to start moving again. None of the children nor the adults wanted to move due to the amount of pain and fear they were experiencing. Jonathon couldn't leave them here either.

The little lights decorated among the brick-tunnel ceiling flickered various shades of yellow and red. It gave off the illusion that there was fire contained within each of the bulbs. It was both terrifying and mystifying to see. *Firelights* was what they used to be called. Since the settlers didn't want to move, Jonathon had taken to staring at them in between his monologues. Thankfully, he wouldn't have to do it much longer. Some of the children decided to take Jonathon up on his offer of introductions and came to sit by him.

There were four of them; among them was Meena. The other three children were older than she was and twice as tall. Out of the other three, only one was male. Jonathon turned his head and looked at each one in stride. The two girls happened to be twins with not a difference between them except for their height. One stood two inches taller than the other. They seated themselves next to Jonathon, holding each other's hands. Their faces were

Sundered

plump and had blue almond-shaped eyes that sparkled from the excitement of being on an adventure. Long curly blonde hair framed their faces, leaving them to appear almost angelic. The girls couldn't be more than nine years old. Despite being covered in dirt and splotches of blood, they appeared perfectly content.

The boy, on the other hand, sat across from Jonathon directly and stared at him cautiously. Compared to the other three, he stood out the most. His face was angular with cuts and bruises, as if he was caught in some kind of neighborhood fight. His hair, pulled back into a small ponytail, was bright and vibrant like the firelights in the tunnel. Even though he was drastically different-looking from the three girls, it wasn't his appearance that made him stand out. It was his eyes. His eyes were the color of the night sky and expressed an unquenchable hatred for the world around him. The boy couldn't be much older than ten, and yet he was already disturbed.

Jonathon shook his head as it dawned on him just how long he had been staring at the boy. Switching gears, he turned his attention to Meena, who had decided to sit next to the boy.

"Hello, Meena. Who's your friends?" Jonathon smiled, trying to be as calm and inviting as possible.

"You don't have to ask her who we are. Why don't you just ask who we are individually?" the boy spoke up, his eyes staring intently at Jonathon. It was enough to send a chill down Jonathon's spine, and he hid his discomfort by taking a deep breath. *This kid...* Not missing a beat, Jonathon addressed the boy directly.

"You're right, I should. And what is your name, little boy?"

"It's Damon Christopher. And I'm not a little boy. I'm a teenager. I'm fourteen years old," the boy answered, hints of anger evident in his voice.

"My apologies...Damon. I guess my powers of observation aren't as potent as they used to be," Jonathon said, trying to sound sincere. *This kid...is awfully small for fourteen. He doesn't look boney...or malnourished. Late bloomer? Recessive-gene lottery?*

Whatever it is, he appears to be quite sensitive to the fact he's rather small. Jonathon turned his head toward the twin girls.

"May I ask what your names are?"

The taller of the twins nodded before responding. "I'm Shana, and this is Monica."

The shorter of the twins waved and smiled.

"All right, thank you all for giving me your names. I already knew Meena's as we had spoken earlier. I'm sure by now you all know my name, and in case you don't, my name is Jonathon Richtor," Jonathon said as he turned his head to look at each of the children.

"Why are you doing this?" Damon asked. His eyebrows were furrowed.

"Well, it's not like we're going anywhere fast down here in the tunnels. I don't know. I was kind of hoping that maybe if we all started talking, motivation could be rekindled so the group would get moving again. That, or if we talk long enough, River would find us."

"Where's Glorious Fish? She's the one that should be looking for us…she wouldn't abandon us…would she? She wouldn't…she loves all of us." It was the shorter of the twins who decided to speak up this time.

Monica looked up at Jonathon with her large blue eyes as if she was waiting for his answer. Her sister, Shana, held her hand as she stared curiously at Damon. Damon in turn continued to stare at Jonathon.

"Glorious Fish made sure we were able to get away safely. Unfortunately, none of us were counting on the mines that the SGPs were so gracious enough to leave us." Jonathon looked between each of the children as he spoke. "She will come back for you. For all of you. She's not the type of woman to leave her people behind. She'll do whatever it takes to make sure you guys are safe. That goes for River too."

Sundered

Jonathon breathed in heavily before pushing himself off the ground and onto his feet. The pains in his ribs were still intense, and try as he may, he could not block it out completely. He stumbled as he got to walking on his feet and placed an arm around his torso to steady himself. The remainder of the Settler's Camp survivors were scattered along the tunnel walls. They all took turns looking at Jonathon as he passed by them. A majority of them looked at him with uncertainty, wondering why a complete stranger would just throw himself into danger willingly. The last few, however, looked at him with annoyance, as if his very presence was the reason for all the strife they'd had to put up with.

Jonathon said nothing more to any of them as he walked down the tunnel away from the group. He was desperate for a cigarette, and he wanted a moment alone to recollect his thoughts. *None of them seem to trust me after the crash. Can I blame them? I'm a complete stranger to them and how they live.*

Jonathon traveled down the tunnel a hundred feet or so before coming to a T intersection. He made a left turn here and traveled twenty more feet before stopping to lean against the right-tunnel wall. There, a section of firelights was dangling from the ceiling; several of the bulbs were busted and jagged to the point of being hooks. Jonathon stared at them as he pulled a cigarette out of his shirt pocket and placed it between his lips. He couldn't imagine what it took to carve the bulbs into hooks, but seeing them dangle in front of him made him feel uneasy.

Jonathon pulled his lighter out of his pocket and was about to light his cigarette when he saw a glint of metal in the distance followed by muzzle fire. The cigarette fell out of his mouth as he dropped to the floor, gasping desperately and rolling to get out of the way of the hail of bullets all flying past him. Hitting the other wall, he hastily crawled his way around the corner as adrenaline began to pour through his body. Heart pounding, he shakily grabbed the Sig Sauer River gave him earlier and ejected the magazine to count how many bullets he had. There were twelve left in the clip. Slamming it back in, he cocked the hammer and took a deep breath in. Closing his eyes, he breathed out slowly while counting in his head. *One…two…three…four…five…*

He opened his eyes and whipped his head and hand around the corner. Relying on his instincts, he squeezed the trigger four times, taking out two of the approaching SGPs. Jonathon hid back around the corner as a hail of bullets took over his former location. *Eight bullets left. Heavy machine fire. Hard to determine how many SGPs there are.*

The machine fire died down, and Jonathon once again rose from his spot. This time, he rolled from his position to the middle of the tunnel hallway on his knees. He fired five more bullets and managed to take out two more SGPs. *Three bullets left.* He counted eight SGPs before having to duck as a bullet whistled over his head. Jonathon rolled back behind the corner as the SGPs opened fire on him again.

"There's no way in hell I'm going to be able to take out all eight with only three bullets left," Jonathon said aloud, breathing heavily. Sweat rolled down his forehead. *I gotta direct them away from the survivors and fast.*

Before he had a chance to act, a familiar voice rang out from behind him.

"RICHTOR." It was River. She was running at full speed toward him.

Oh thank god. Jonathon snapped his head toward her direction and noticed there was someone else running behind River. It was the guy who had been driving the quad. They were both unscathed.

"RIVER! SGPs DOWN THE LEFT TUNNEL!" Jonathon shouted to her.

River nodded as she heard the message. She turned her head briefly to say something to the man who was running next to her before breaking off and running alongside the other wall. The man slowed his pace and bunkered down in the middle of the tunnel.

Sundered

What happened next left Jonathon completely bewildered. River slid past him completely unarmed.

"Sniper directive," River said just as she reached the far wall. She swung her right leg in front of her as it shape-shifted into a sniper rifle and began firing. She muttered something to herself, and the sniper rifle she was wielding reconfigured itself back into her leg. Using both legs, she kicked off the wall and flipped herself over back to her feet. Machine-gun fire followed shortly after River as she dashed around down the hallway.

"Deflection directive!" River shouted.

Jonathon turned his head around the corner and watched as River deflected all the shots the SGPs were taking at her using her metal arm. The way she moved was something out of an action movie. Graceful and yet reckless. After dodging yet another hail of bullets, she slid underneath one of the SGPs, knocking him over at the knees before stealing his gun and continuing her assault.

Jonathon was floored. He turned away from the corner and toward the man who was with River.

"What the hell? Since when has she been able to do this?"

"Couldn't tell you, mate. Until today, I didn't even know anything about her.

"She's like a one-man army. It's incredible."

"I take it you know her well?" the man looked at Jonathon with interest.

"Indeed. Or at least I used to. I'm afraid we're mere acquaintances now."

"Mere, eh? Sounds complicated." The man chuckled. "Name's Wickler. I was assigned to be her driver for this expedition." He stuck his hand out before Jonathon.

"Jonathon Richtor," Jonathon answered as he shook his hand. "I suppose we should swap some stories later."

"Looking forward to it, mate, but for now, we better get the lass and the rest of the others out of here."

"Agreed." Jonathon nodded. "Tell me, you know how to use that?" Jonathon pointed toward the machine gun wrapped around Wickler.

"Aye. Don't you worry. I trust you have a weapon of your own?"

"I do. It's the Sig that River handed to me earlier today. However, I don't have much ammo left for it," Jonathon said. Something dawned on him as he said the last few words. *River handed me the Sig...but didn't she give me additional magazine clips with it? She did, didn't she? So where did I put them?* Jonathon began to pad himself down as he struggled to remember where he placed the clips. He stopped as he felt their shape in his pants' side pocket.

"Never mind, I've got plenty for the time being," Jonathon said confidently as he ejected the magazine and reloaded. Wickler nodded. Jonathon pointed toward the corner with two fingers. Wickler nodded once more and followed suit behind him as he turned around the corner.

25

There he is.

Glorious Fish watched patiently from behind the tree as she continued to stare at Mustang. The mech had done nothing since slaughtering its entire unit. It just stood there, staring at the sky.

How close can I get before it notices me?

She crept down low and quietly made her way over to the next set of trees.

No movement still. Is it possible that it powered down in some form?

Glorious Fish made it to the trees and placed her back flat against the largest one. She peered around the tree. Kirran and Tiny George were both making their way toward him. Kirran had taken to approaching the opposite side of Glorious Fish while Tiny George made his way toward the rear. As they still didn't know what they were dealing with exactly or if there was a human being piloting the mechanized unit, Glorious Fish thought it was absolutely necessary to approach the metal beast with complete discretion.

There's got to be some kind of life within that hulking giant, although I doubt we would be able to persuade them. The machinery would be a win for us if we could get our hands on it though.

Glorious Fish pushed away from the large tree just as the Tilithe triangle began to chirp loudly within her pocket.

SHIT!

Mustang reacted almost instantly. Glorious Fish immediately dove forward and rolled away as a saw blade soared behind her, taking out the tree she was using as refuge.

Who the hell is calling now!

"plan b!" Glorious Fish shouted as she took off in a mad sprint away from Mustang. The Tilithe still continued to chirp. She angrily pulled it out of her pocket and answered it. "Not to sound rude, but this is absolutely not a good frigging time."

"Why? What's wrong?" Xavier responded.

"Frosty? Unless you're magically going to appear with air support, there's no point in telling you where we are." Glorious Fish stopped short as a saw blade flew in front of her. The second one clipped her in the shoulder as it whizzed behind her.

"What is that noise? Projectiles of some sort? I can help. Where are you?" Xavier sounded excited.

"Same place…our caravan was in. Just a little further…in…," Glorious Fish said through gritted teeth. "If you're coming, come already. I've already been hit….Gaahh, I need to keep running." She ended the call and pocketed the Tilithe immediately. *Focus. Don't let this thing hit you twice.* Sucking in air, she broke off into a dead run.

Glorious Fish heard Tiny George and Kirran shout somewhere behind her, but she couldn't make out what they were saying exactly. She turned her head over her shoulder and saw that Mustang had diverted its attention to the other two. She watched wide-eyed as Tiny George took another saw blade to his shoulder, and he dropped to the ground. She switched directions and began running headfirst toward Mustang. Reaching into one of her back pouches, she pulled out one of the EMP grenades. Mustang, as if sensing her approaching presence, turned back toward her and began to open fire on her with its miniguns.

Focus, focus! Glorious Fish held her breath briefly as she danced around the field, dodging the bullet stream as she went along. *FOCUS!* In one swift motion, she primed the EMP, threw it,

Sundered

and then threw herself forward toward one of the tree clusters. Mustang let off one last hail of bullets toward her location before looking down at the EMP. It went off with a brilliant flash of light, instantly paralyzing the hulking metal giant. A loud deafening scream emanated from somewhere inside it, and it fell to the ground, unable to defend itself any further.

Glorious Fish peered around the corner from the trees, breathing heavily. She watched closely for a few seconds, waiting to see if it would move. Thankfully, it did not. The EMP grenade did its job. She wiped her brow in relief and then began to feel a sharp pain on her side. Glorious Fish looked down and saw blood rapidly spreading under her shirt. She lifted it and saw a bullet hole somewhere over her intestines.

"Just my luck." Glorious Fish pushed off the tree and brought herself to her feet. She walked around the trees and toward the metal giant paralyzed on the ground. She looked around as she did, looking for signs of her hunters. "Kirran! Tiny George!" she called out, waiting patiently for an answer. Two minutes went by before she called out again. "Hey! Are you two all right?"

"Fish! Here! Nnngh…," Tiny George called out weakly.

"Fish! Tiny George took a pretty big hit," Kirran called out next. His voice rang out from the same area as Tiny George.

Glorious Fish headed off toward their direction, turning every so often to check on Mustang. She didn't have to walk far as they were making their way toward her. Tiny George was slumped up against Kirran, using him as a support as they continued to make their way. Tiny George was a mess. The saw blade she had seen him take to the shoulder earlier was not quite his shoulder. The saw blade had cut cleanly through his skin and bone, taking his left arm in the middle of his bicep. The saw blade had also managed to cut into his chest, taking a portion of the flesh with it.

"Tiny George. My dear, we need to get you immediate medical attention…Xavier Frost should be on his way." Glorious

Fish walked to his other side and put his good arm around her shoulders and walked him toward Mustang.

"It's just a...flesh wound, boss...barely a scratch, really," Tiny George said between breaths.

"If you think this is just a scratch, dear boy, I'd love to see what you consider a real wound then. Otherwise, we should update our definitions." Glorious Fish chuckled. "No, no, sweet George, we'll have the good doctor patch you up. Just hold out on us a little longer."

"Can we assume he's coming here by air? If so, he's pretty close...look there! It's a helicopter." Kirran nodded toward the horizon.

"Well, I'll be. I didn't know the good doctor had a helicopter—wait, is that even a helicopter?" Glorious Fish said as she stared at the approaching aircraft.

As it flew closer to where they stood, they realized it was not what they originally thought. To call the contraption he was flying a helicopter would be extremely inaccurate. It looked closer to a boat with metal wings attached to it or a dirigible without the balloon envelope. Glorious Fish had no idea what possessed Xavier to create such a thing, but she was certainly glad he did. Glorious Fish couldn't help but laugh as the contraption loomed ever closer. Decorated in various shades of yellow and blue, the metal surrounding the aircraft was twisted and contorted in such shapes that it made it appear like a colorful skeleton. It was an impressive, if not goofy, sight.

Glorious Fish stepped forward to meet Xavier as he landed and stepped off his aircraft, not even moments later.

"Frosty! What manner of metal beast is this?" Glorious Fish asked as she motioned for Kirran to bring Tiny George forward.

"Fish. I call it the Skywatch. It's a combination of technologies new and old. I found an old military blueprint a long while back and made some necessary modifications and alterations of my own design. That aside, who needs medical attention?" Xavier looked Glorious Fish over before looking at Tiny George as Kirran carried him forward. "Holy hell, you look like you were caught in a lawn mower. What happened? Never mind that. Get him up on the Skywatch. There's a cabin on the backside. Half of it is dedicated to a lab. I should have enough equipment on board that'll be able to fix him up." Xavier nodded and walked back onto the Skywatch and toward the cabin.

"You heard the good doctor, Kirran. Let's get Tiny George on this…strange thing." Glorious Fish helped Kirran lead Tiny George onto the deck of the Skywatch.

"I can take him into the lab, Fish, if you want to check on Mustang out there. Can't be much longer before the EMP wears off. We don't need him coming after us again," Kirran said as he readjusted Tiny George to lean against him better.

"Ooooh, good point. All right, Kirran, help Frosty patch up our George. I'll let you guys know what I find." Glorious Fish lightly patted Tiny George on the back before walking away. He, in turn, managed a small smile in passing before his face contorted back into pain.

Glorious Fish walked off the Skywatch keeping even pace. Consciously aware that there wasn't much time before Mustang would be free of its paralysis, she checked her side pouch to make sure she had the other EMP grenade. Satisfied it was still tucked away securely, Glorious Fish made a straight beeline for the downed metal giant.

26

"See if you can get them motivated to move. I tried earlier and well…as you can see, we didn't get very far. I'll scout ahead and make sure there's no other stragglers left in the tunnels," Jonathon said as he slid his last spare magazine into the Sig Sauer.

"Why can't you just stick with the group? I don't have a way of being able to contact you once you go wandering around down here." River looked at him, shaking her head.

"Just trying to avoid further surprises is all. I should be all right to scout ahead." Jonathon raised an eyebrow at her.

"I'm gonna go ahead here and just tell you no. We're low on ammo, and almost everyone here is injured in one form or another. Including you. Don't think for one second I won't knock you flat on your ass if you try to scout ahead anyways."

"Sheesh…all right, all right. I'll wait until we can get the group moving." Jonathon threw his hands up in the air, accepting defeat.

"Good. Now sit tight." River walked away from Jonathon and toward the settlers huddled up along the walls of the tunnel. Wickler, who had been waiting patiently on the side, followed behind her.

"Everyone, we need to get going. Now! The SGPs are hot on our trail, and we're only about halfway to the Axler," River shouted.

"All right, mates, you heard the gal. She's no stranger to any of us. So right then, off your taints and let's be off," Wickler shouted

Sundered

after her. "Logan, where are you, love?" A small dark-haired boy rose from his spot by the far side of the tunnel and got excited as he saw him drew near. Wickler met him halfway and pulled him into his arms.

Numerous complaints rifled throughout the survivors of the Settler's Camp. River looked at all their faces as they continued to make their objections. Even though none of them had life-threatening injuries, most of them acted with great reluctance, as if their personal safety was becoming more and more an inconvenience. *That's odd. Usually the settlers have way more gusto. Did the latest events cause them to lose their zest for life? That seems highly unusual—wait a second.*

"Are you guys all reluctant to move because Glorious Fish isn't here?" River shouted, a little louder this time, to make sure all of the settlers heard her. Confirmations rang out across the tunnel along with nodding of their heads. An angry familiar-looking teenager appeared before River. It was Damon, his red hair shining vividly under the firelights.

"Where is she? Did you leave her to die?" Damon asked, sizing her up and down. "I swear to god, River, if you left her to die—"

"Cool it, Damon," River said as calmly as she could while cutting him off. "Fish isn't likely to die so easily. You, of all people, should know that."

"Prove it! Prove to me that you didn't leave her to die!" Damon said in a high voice.

River's eyes narrowed on Damon as he stared up at her defiantly. Without taking her eyes off him, she removed the Tilithe triangle from one of her side pouches and brought it before him. Flicking the top of the triangle back with her thumb, she called Glorious Fish. A few seconds passed before she answered.

"Fish, are you there?"

"River, darling, is that you? Did you find my settlers?" Glorious Fish's face filled the void above the triangle.

"Yeah, Fish, I'm standing right in front of them. They don't seem to want to travel much anymore. They're all too busy worrying about you."

"Is that so? Are you close enough to them that they can hear me?"

"Yep. Damon especially." River stepped forward closer to the settlers. Damon walked with her, staring wide-eyed at the Tilithe.

"Good. Listen here, lovelies, you need to follow our wonderful River Rutherford to safety. She wants nothing more than to keep you alive and well. Trust me when I say that. All of you will see me again, you can count on that. But there's a few things over here I need to tie up before I'm able to meet up with you guys. Including, but not limited to, getting the good doctor here to patch up Tiny George and myself, tame this ridiculous mechanized unit whom I've affectionately named Mustang, and make sure there's no other SGPs in the area that will follow us back to base." Glorious Fish paused for a moment and began to breathe heavily.

"Mom! Mom! Are you all right?" Damon jumped up and whipped the Tilithe right out of River's hands.

"Yes, child, I'm all right. Don't worry. Whooo…just needed a moment to breathe. Running and all that. It's been…a rather big handful over here. But nothing I can't handle, so don't you worry," Glorious said as she took long breaths between sentences.

"You wouldn't lie to me…would you? You wouldn't lie to me like my real parents, would you?" Damon voice began to tremble.

"Damon, dear, I have never lied to you and don't intend to do so now. I promise you, I will see you and everyone else back at the Axler. Now, will you promise me one thing? Will you listen to everything that River tells you?"

"Yes, ma'am…I'll listen to River, but you better be at the Axler or else!" Damon tossed the Tilithe to River and walked away.

"I see Damon is still as charming as ever," River said as she brought the Tilithe to her face.

Sundered

"He does have his moments. Do keep him safe for me, River. He's the closest thing I have to a son. And it goes without saying to keep my settlers safe as well. Now get going! We both have things we need to get done." Glorious Fish said nothing further and waited a moment before cutting the line.

River turned her attention toward the settlers. "You heard her. Now does anyone still have an objection to getting out of this tunnel? No? Good. Now let's go." River waved her metal arm in a circle and used her other arm to point them forward. "Come on, guys, I know you're tough. I've seen you in worse shape than this."

With no other objections holding them back, the settlers began to move as a group through the tunnel. Once they were moving, River motioned for Wickler to come over.

"Hey, would you be able to follow behind the group? I would, but I'm the only one who knows the way out of these tunnels, and I want to make sure no SGPs are going to be able to take us out from behind," River whispered to him.

"No problem. Mind if I keep me boy with me?" Wickler whispered back to her.

"Feel free, just be careful."

Wickler nodded to her and called out for Logan to come stand with him before moving behind

the group. River then proceeded to make her way ahead of the group, tapping Jonathon on the shoulder and then beckoning him to follow her.

"Do you, by any chance, know how to get out of these tunnels?" he asked.

"Yeah, I think I'm the only one who does. 'Course, it's been a few years since I was in here last."

"Willingly? Eh—never mind."

"Not exactly. Anyways, I need you to stay with the group at all times. I may need to scout ahead in a few tunnels to make sure we're going in the right direction."

"Is this why you didn't want me scouting off by myself earlier?"

"Partially. The pathway out is kind of tricky. That, and there's two tunnels that are lined with all kinds of booby traps."

"What the…? What the hell were these tunnels used for?" Jonathon shook his head.

"Honestly? I don't know. No one else has been down here in several decades, or as far as I know anyhow. I couldn't even begin to tell you about the traps that are down here. They look like they came before my time," River said, shrugging her shoulders.

Jonathon shook his head some more, and they continued on down the tunnels in silence. River was very careful and meticulous when determining which turns to take. *Left. Left. Right. Right. No, no…gotta go back. Left. Left again. Straight path.* They only had to double-back once, and thankfully, there were no other surprises hiding for them in the tunnels. The settlers themselves didn't complain as they continued to listen and follow River. Damon himself walked directly behind her.

Finally, after three hours in the tunnels, River was able to lead them outside. The children all exclaimed in excitement, happy to be out in open air, Damon among them. The sky appeared a pale yellow against the clouds that were forming. Daybreak was upon them. Seeing the color yellow, especially in the sky, was something out of the norm these days. Everywhere else you went in Sunderi, the sky appeared monochromatic.

"You know, I don't understand how the sky actually has color over here," Jonathon said as he looked up at the sky.

"I don't either. 'Course, I don't think either of us knows why everywhere else has turned devoid of color to begin with," River said, looking around. "All right, guys. Small break time. It's not that much farther away."

Everyone, save for River and Jonathon, sat down from where they stood. Jonathon broke away from the group and walked toward the cliffs that surrounded the left side of the tunnel exit. River watched him as he pulled a bent cigarette out of his pocket and put it between his lips. She turned her head to look back at the settlers just as Jonathon began to rummage through his pockets looking for something else. River closed her eyes and breathed out slowly. *Whew. Thankfully, there were no other surprises waiting for us in the tunnels.* She began to feel herself relax, and her thoughts began to drift. *Xavier…will you be there when we arrive at the Axler? Will you be mad that I'm in one piece this time?*

Something began to feel off, and River snapped open her eyes. The settlers in front of her were all still engaged among themselves and had no sense of urgency. River turned her head to look over at Jonathon. He was gone!

"Jonathon?" she said as she ran over to the cliffs where she had seen him previously. There was a lighter on the ground. *He dropped his lighter? Did he walk off somewhere?* River scooped it up and examined her surroundings closer. The cliffs were aged and battered by high winds and yet, at the same time, showed signs of a struggle. She stood up and looked over the edge of the cliff. There was Jonathon and a lone SGP covered in complete combat gear. The SGP had just succeeded in knocking Jonathon down to his knees and was raising a shotgun to his chest. Without thinking, River jumped off the cliff.

"Deflection directive!" she shouted just before landing between them. Her metal arm instinctively went up and covered her face as the SGP squeezed the trigger. Her metal arm absorbed the impact from the buckshot, recoiling and stopping just short of her face. Dropping down, River swung her legs out in front of her, tripping the SGP. Flat on his back, the SGP aimed his shotgun toward River and fired again. Her arm went in front of her face again as she pulled a combat knife out of the sheath on her waist. River felt something go over her head, and she plunged forward as fast as she could toward the SGP and drove the knife right through his face. He was dead.

Hearing a gasp behind her, she turned her head to look. Jonathon was pointing and staring at her, pale as a ghost.

"What's wrong? Are you hurt?" River asked, concerned she wasn't able protect him.

"I'm fine...but...but your head! You're bleesding!"

"I'm what?" River pushed herself away from the SGP and onto her feet. Using her left hand, she felt along the topside of her head. Sharp pains began to pierce through the top of her head, and she ran her fingers over that particular area before bringing it down before her face. Blood. Lots of blood.

"Holy shit...," she said, looking at it. Something in her stomach began to churn, and everything about her began to feel heavy. With the adrenaline dying down, River no longer had the strength to hold herself up and began to fall over.

"River?" Jonathon stepped forward and caught her as she was falling. "river!" He started to shake her. "Oh Christ. WICKLER! SOMEBODY! RIVER'S HIT! Oh jeez...River! Open your eyes! OPEN YOUR EYES!"

27

Hmm, I wonder what's inside Mustang.

Glorious Fish walked slowly around Mustang. She had already walked around it several times but still continued to do so in hopes of finding a way of opening it up. So far, there had been no luck. Noting a small tinted visor on the front side of its "face," Glorious Fish climbed up Mustang to get in front of it. She placed her hands above her eyes as she leaned in close to the visor. Glorious Fish could vaguely make out a silhouette of a person on the inside but nothing else. She began to knock on the visor. No response. She tried again. This time, she was met with a muffled scream.

"Is anyone in there?" Glorious Fish peered into the visor again. She could no longer make out the individual who was in there. Before long, Glorious Fish began to hear pounding coming from the inside of the mech.

"Ah, someone is in there! All right, here's the deal. I'll help get you out, but you better not attack me. Because I guarantee…you won't like it if you do," Glorious Fish shouted, hoping the man or whoever it was inside could hear her.

She climbed back down the metal giant and made her way around it. A noise akin to air being released was heard as she made her around to the top side. Yet there was nothing there that could project such a sound. *What the hell was that just now?*

Glorious Fish searched around the top plate of the mechanized unit looking for some way to get inside. No dice. Just as she was about to turn her head to look elsewhere, a glint caught her eye. Squatting down, she noticed a valve tucked in between the shoulder joint and the minigun on the left side of the mech.

Yeah, there was no way of seeing that previously, she thought. *Wait, shouldn't the effects of the EMP grenade worn off by now? Well, this oughta be rather dangerous then...oh, what a treat.* Glorious Fish laughed to herself as she began to turn the valve. *Hope Tiny George is going to be all right. And then there's Damon to consider. That boy...*

Glorious Fish continued to rotate the valve until it wouldn't any further. The sound of air being released was heard once again, and this time, Glorious Fish could see it. Once all the air was released from its chamber, a loud *pfiiiish* sounded afterward, followed by a cloud of smoke coming from the face of the mechanized unit. Glorious Fish climbed back up Mustang toward the visor. She could see the outline of an opening below the visor. Digging her fingers in, she pulled back on the plate, expecting it to be rather thick and heavy to move. Surprisingly enough, it moved with little difficulty. At closer inspection, she realized she had found the door that allowed someone to get inside the mechanized unit and that the door was operated by hydraulics.

Before Glorious Fish was able to move around the door to peer inside, a young man emerged, coughing heavily. Stumbling, the young man couldn't keep his balance and fell off Mustang. He hit the ground with a loud thud and rolled onto his back. Glorious Fish jumped off afterward and walked a few steps so she could stand over him. The man was rather scrawny, almost to the point of being nothing but bones. Cuts and bruises covered his arms. Glorious Fish guesstimated he had to be around twenty years old and maybe 5"9' or 5"10'. He had brown shoulder-length hair, and his eyes, despite being the color green, were dull and lifeless. Glorious Fish was shocked at the fact that the poor man was still breathing. Wanting to be cautious, she bent down to check him for weapons.

"Don't move," she said as she started her search.

"Please…please don't make me go back in there," the young man whimpered.

"Trust me, I have no desire to do so, darling…you've caused enough destruction out here," Glorious Fish responded, satisfied she found nothing on his person.

"No…more…no…more," the young man began to cry and turned on his side.

"No more…? Look, I'm not going to hurt you. Well, I won't hurt you as long as you don't try something stupid anyhow. Look at me," Glorious Fish said as she stepped to his right side and bent back down to his level. "I can get you medical attention and food, but you gotta talk to me, bud. Okay? Do you understand me?"

The young man nodded before sobbing some more. "Just don't make me get back into the machine."

"I won't, I promise. What's your name, darling?"

"Matthew…I think. The officers kept referring to me as Parodius 12."

"Officers?" Glorious Fish asked, raising an eyebrow.

"Yes, the *officers*. They said I couldn't eat nor get out of that thing unless I made my kill count," Matthew responded, pointing at Mustang without looking at it. His tears began to subside a bit.

Glorious Fish's eyes narrowed. She knew the SGPs routinely went out on patrols to hunt down their targets, but this was thought to be because they had designated targets still being generated from the government. *Is there something else at play here?*

"Matthew, how was the kill count measured? Did they give you a list of targets you were supposed to take down?"

"No. They just told us if we wanted to live, we needed to take down the rebels so there wouldn't be any interference to the grand plan." Matthew rolled onto his back. He reached his arm up to the sky, spreading his fingertips. "The sky…even as gray as it is…I still wish I could touch it."

"I have more questions to ask you, but I'd feel more comfortable if I could get you patched up first. Can you walk, son?" Glorious Fish asked, reaching her hand out in front of him.

"I don't really know…they used to stick us in the machines for weeks at a time."

"I'll help you. Here. Hold on to me." Glorious Fish pulled him to his feet and wrapped his arm around her shoulder.

"I'm sorry…I'm so sorry. I didn't want to do those things… but they said they would kill us if we didn't…," Matthew began to sob once more.

"Hey, hey…it's okay. I know you're in pain, but you gotta relax. Come on, let's get you somewhere safe." With Matthew in tow, Glorious Fish started walking forward.

"Hey. Why are you helping me? Aren't I a bad guy to you?"

"Somewhat. If you had come out of that mech, guns ablazing, we wouldn't be having this conversation. However, since you were incapable of defending yourself, I decided to take pity on you. Should I regret doing so?" Glorious Fish turned her head to look at him.

"No…I'm glad you did. I've been wanting freedom away for so long…I miss my dad and my aunt. I really hope they're still alive."

"What's your dad's name? Maybe I know him."

"Jonathon. Jonathon Richtor."

28

"Madison, please. Eat something." Claire stared at Madison, concerned.

"I can't...I don't like peas," Madison said as she pushed the peas around her plate.

"You ate them just fine a couple days ago. Are they not the same as always?" Tempest looked around the table, confused.

"The peas are fine, Tempest," Brad said without looking up from his plate. "She's probably having a side effect from the nanomachines. It's a rare side effect, but it's been known to happen to patients with...slow development."

"Are you trying to say I'm an invalid? I'll have you know I'm a mastermind when it comes to computers." Madison narrowed her eyes on Brad, irritability rising.

"Chill out," Brad said, trying to finish chewing his peas. "Slow development as in a body that develops in a much slower state, usually due to an underlying medical condition. Which you've had for many years."

Madison continued to stare at Brad awhile longer before returning back to her plate and pushing her peas around.

The atmosphere at the Jamessons had been difficult to bear with. Claire was becoming more and more overbearing, secretly trying to give her injections full of vitamins and other supplements. Brad, on the other hand, observed her and monitored her progress every day and continuously made up excuses why she was changing. Her taste buds were just the latest victim in her body's "late" development.

Madison prayed hard every day, hoping Jonathon would be back soon. She couldn't wait to get away from her sister. *Maybe it's a good thing she didn't visit often after all. Gosh, I wouldn't want to put up with her every day for the past eighteen years. I think I would have gone mad!*

And then there was Tempest. Tempest had continued to treat her just the same, even after that night of being temporarily paralyzed. He even was a source of comfort to her, especially during the times of Claire's mood swings of affection. It was a relief to say the least.

Not wanting to upset him, Madison scooped up some peas with her mashed potatoes and began to chew quickly. She hoped that eating them together would disguise the taste. It worked for the most part, and she was able to clear her plate of peas with minor disgust.

Tempest beamed at her pleased.

"The peas are tolerable then, Ms. Madison?"

"Not really. Didn't want them going to waste though. Next time…can we try something without peas?" Madison looked at Tempest apologetically.

"I suppose we could actually," Tempest said, stroking his chin. "I believe we have corn and some sweet potatoes left. Which reminds me." He turned to face Brad. "Mr. Jamesson, I need your permission to go hunt down more gardening supplies. The soil down here is becoming rather difficult as of late. I fear we may need an actual irrigation system."

Brad raised an eyebrow at Tempest's request. He began to drum his fingers along the corner of the table. Before long, he leaned back into his chair and looked first at Claire and then back over to Tempest.

"Are you going to travel into Arcturus?" Brad asked.

Sundered

"Where else would I buy the best gardening supplies?" Tempest responded, smiling.

"Smart ass. How do you plan to pay for them?"

"By stealing them, of course. Nothing says free like a five-finger discount!" Tempest laughed.

Brad scowled and shook his head. Eyeing his expression, Tempest instantly stopped laughing.

"My apologies, Mr. Jamesson. It seems my humor is misplaced. I fully intend to pay for the supplies needed with some of the cash we have left over."

"What is Arcturus?" Madison piped up, curious. Brad, Claire, and Tempest looked over at her.

"It's a city. Have you never heard of it?" Claire looked at her.

"No…I've literally spent the last ten years underground with Jonathon and Matthew. I…really didn't get to go outside much or travel. Jonathon usually made the trips alone, or sometimes, someone would show up and drop off supplies and clothes for us." Madison looked at everyone. "What? Is there something I'm missing here?"

"You may be missing out on a lot actually. Do you know why you guys lived underground?" Brad leaned forward in his seat.

"Jonathon said it wasn't safe on the surface. Especially with my condition."

"It's not. My god. Although, you probably weren't old enough to care about what was going on in the world. Well…you were what?" Brad pointed at her.

"Fourteen."

"Okay, fourteen. You probably had no interest in what was going on in politics or with the government."

"That's not entirely accurate," Madison said. "I followed most of what was going on before Jon moved us underground. There was a big buzz on the undernet about what the government was planning."

"There was more than just a big buzz, Ms. Madison. The entire undernet was on fire about what was going to happen." Tempest looked at her, surprised. "Law enforcement everywhere couldn't take what they found seriously. They refused to believe the government would do something so drastic. Which was ridiculous, considering how much of their plan was leaked."

Madison's eyes widened. "Yeah, I remember the news segments they ran during that time. They claimed it was the survivalists paranoia catching up with them."

"Indeed. They did all kinds of things to keep it under wraps. Surprisingly enough, no media outlet wanted to touch the subject." Tempest nodded.

"If I had to guess, it was because of fear. People do all sorts of weird things when they're scared," Brad chimed in.

"Right. Millions of people were killed over the span of the past decade. Jon used to keep a tally. As a matter of fact, he kept an entire series of journals chronicling the events of the massacres and the events that surrounded it. He used to tell me all the time that it was important to keep an accurate account of everything that happened and is happening so that one day society could rebuild itself," Madison said. She found herself wondering why the government took the measures it did. *None of it makes sense.*

"Back on topic here. You asked what Arcturus was. As was already stated, it's a city. It's one of three untouched cities." Brad placed his hands on the table. "Reason why we call it untouched is because it's literally that. The government has done nothing to it. There's people who still live there, and they go about their everyday lives without a care in the world. 'Course, the people there also seem to think the government is going out of their way to protect them from the riffraff of the world. In other words, people like us."

"And Tempest wants to go there to get gardening supplies? Why does this scream all kinds of dangerous to me? Wouldn't they try to attack him?" Madison's eyes widened once again.

"Heavens, no. I'm considered a regular there. As long as I have cash, they don't tend to ask too many questions. Besides, would anyone truly attack someone over gardening supplies?" Tempest said, cracking a smile. Madison narrowed her eyes and scowled at Tempest's attitude at the whole thing.

"I think we should all go. It would be nice to get some air for once," Claire said as she got up from her seat. She looked directly over at Brad and held his gaze.

"Fine. But if we need to bail for whatever reason, nobody better question why and just do it. While we're there, it would be nice to pick up other supplies we need," Brad said before getting up from the table and walking into the next room.

Madison sat at the table awhile longer and watched as Claire and Tempest began to clear the table. After receiving a few odd looks from Claire, she got up and proceeded to help them finish cleaning up the rest. When all the dishes were gathered and the table was wiped down, Madison pulled Tempest aside.

"Be honest with me. Is Arcturus dangerous, Tempest?" Madison scanned his face, looking for an answer.

"Ms. Madison, walking around on the surface is far more dangerous than the city of Arcturus." Tempest smiled. "But don't worry, by the power vested in me as an appointed assistant, I shall make it my life's goal to keep you out of harm's way." With that said, he winked and left Madison standing there, uncertain of what to make of his words.

29

Jonathon wiped the sweat from his brow and readjusted River over his shoulder for the seventh time. The heat of the day was beginning to wear down hard on him, especially with the additional weight he needed to carry. Breezes drifted along as he walked, but they were only temporarily relief against the climbing humidity.

"Cripes. It's getting really sticky." Jonathon panted.

"You can say that again, mate. It feels like the humidity has raised another 20 percent. It's making it mighty uncomfortable in the nether regions." Wickler nodded before pointing down below.

"We're going to need to switch off pretty soon, Wick," Jonathon said, trying to ignore the heat.

"Getting tired, ya?"

"Yeah, and I need to reassess where we are. And maybe find some shade…or something." Jonathon groaned as he pulled River off his shoulder and handed her over to Wickler. "Oh, relief! My ribs. Thank you, my friend."

Wickler chuckled at him as he swung River over his left shoulder. Wickler had been a source of comic relief for Jonathon throughout this leg of the journey. Between swapping war stories and old childhood memories, it seemed like neither of them could run out of things to talk about. Due to the times River had saved him in the past and just prior at the exit from the tunnels,

Sundered

Jonathon had opted to carry her himself. Despite how much his ribs screamed at him, he pressed on, readjusting her as needed. That was until Wickler suggested to him that they both trade off carrying her to avoid getting overexerted.

With three additional hours under their belts, Jonathon wondered how much further they were from the Axler. Surveying the land, he spotted several large trees and poles in the distance.

"Looks like there's a road over yonder," Jonathon said as he pointed out into the distance.

Wickler raised his hand over his eyes. "Aye, that it does. Were we supposed to keep an eye out for a road?"

"Good question. Hey, she was able to talk to someone with that that triangle thing, wasn't she? Do you suppose we could get ahold of someone to make sure we're going in the right direction?" Jonathon said, stopping in front of Wickler.

"Worth a try. You'll have to search her person though."

"Won't require a ton of searching. She's only got those belt pouches," Jonathon said, nodding to himself. *If River knew I was checking her pockets while she was unconscious, she would be absolutely livid. However, considering the circumstances, I hope she'll forgive me.*

He found the Tilithe triangle nestled in the third pouch on her belt and removed it delicately.

"This is it, right? The thing she was talking through earlier?"

"Looks like it. Don't ask me how it works though. I wasn't standing that close when she used it."

Jonathon turned it over, trying to figure out how it worked. He noticed a line that went around one tip of the triangle. Feeling along the line, he realized the tip flipped back. *What now? Can't input numbers or anything. If I recall correctly, River just said a name to it. I'll try that.*

"Uh…Glorious Fish," he said aloud to the triangle. A minute passed before Glorious Fish's familiar holographic face appeared.

"Jonathon?" Glorious Fish asked, confused.

"Hey…Glorious Fish…uh…listen—," Jonathon started.

"Where's River?"

"About that. She's with us...however, she's unconscious. She was—"

"What happened? You wouldn't try to do something funny now, would you?"

"No! Look, listen, damnit. I'll explain to you what happened and why we're calling if you stop interrupting," Jonathon shouted.

A few seconds of silence passed by before she spoke again.

"I'm listening."

"Good. All right. We're somewhere beyond the underground tunnels and a road surrounded by trees and poles. We have no idea how far we are from the Axler. River was leading us up until a few hours ago, but thanks to an unexpected rogue SGP, she's now unconscious, and we're guideless."

"What do you mean unexpected rogue SGP?" Glorious Fish raised an eyebrow. "River doesn't just let single targets get the surprise on her."

"It was unexpected because...the SGP made a jump on me while I was retrieving my cigarette, and she intervened, saving my life while also causing herself to go unconscious. She blocked two plasma shotgun blasts." Jonathon swallowed hard.

"My god, Jonathon! Can you not travel with women and avoid getting into trouble? Honestly," Glorious Fish exclaimed.

"I have my days...what do you expect out of a discredited reporter?"

Another voice could be heard through the Tilithe. Jonathon couldn't quite make out what he was saying, but Glorious Fish responded to him just the same. She eventually turned her attention back to Jonathon.

"All right. Thanks to everyone's favorite mad scientist, we now have a type of air vessel. We should be able to find you guys and scoop you up for the rescue."

"Really? That would definitely help your settlers here. They've been holding themselves pretty good since that pep talk you gave them," Jonathon said, relieved.

"They better. Otherwise, they're gonna be due for some extra loving. And not the nice kind." Glorious Fish laughed.

"Right. Uh, when should we expect you?"

"The good doctor here just identified your location, so we should be there in about twenty minutes."

"Great, we'll see—"

"And Jonathon, don't you dare let her die," a deep voice called out over the Tilithe.

Jonathon didn't recognize it. *Could this be the good doctor?* "It's not my intention to do so. 'Course, it wasn't my intention to let her take a few bullets for me either."

"Keep it that way. Otherwise, you're going to find yourself on my operating table," the deep voice called out before cutting the connection.

Jonathon pushed the tip back on to the triangle and shuddered. That last message was enough to put a chill down his spine. Whoever he was, he definitely did not want to piss him off. Shaking off the goosebumps that were developing, Jonathon replaced the Tilithe back into River's belt pouch.

"Ooooh, mate. The good doctor that Glorious Fish was referring to was Xavier Frost. He's bloody brilliant. However, he's also a bit crazed. Whatever you do, do not piss him off." Wickler whistled before shaking his head.

"Trust me, I do not want to," Jonathon said before turning his attention to the survivors. "All right, listen up, guys! Your beloved…leader is on her way here with an aircraft of sorts. She is going to be taking us the rest of the way to safety."

Excited voices rang out among the survivors.

"Hurray!"

"We're saved!"

"No more of this heat!"

One by one the survivors all began to sit down where they stood. Jonathon couldn't help but make a comparison to how a dog acted when it was told to sit. Trying not to chuckle, he turned back toward Wickler and helped lower River off his shoulder and onto the ground.

30

River woke with a start.

Where am I?

She looked around her surroundings and gasped. *This is my room! How did I get back here?* A number of thoughts raced through River's mind as she sat upright and began to move about her room. *What happened exactly? I remember jumping in front of Jonathon...and then everything is blank. And my head...it feels like it's going to split open.*

River struggled with the overwhelming urge to scratch her arm. *What is this? Since when did I get these types of sensations?*

Xavier entered the room and watched as River clutched her mechanical arm. She fumbled with it as if she was trying to tear it off. She grew frustrated after a while and gave up. Xavier cleared his throat to let his presence be known.

River turned around and grew wide-eyed as she realized who was standing there. "Xavier! Where the hell have you been?" she exclaimed, trying to keep her pain from her voice.

Xavier looked at her curiously as she tried to stand confidently.

"Your chip is malfunctioning. Wait, Fish did mention a head wound. She must have meant you."

River scowled and then nodded as the pain intensified.

"I really wish you would be more honest with me, River. Your stubbornness is becoming rather unbecoming of you. Honestly, if you're not careful, you're going to get yourself killed. And then what would I do? I would have no one to annoy or tinker with."

"Oh, I'm sure you'd be heartbroken. 'Course, probably not for long, considering how much you love dead bodies."

"Ouch." Xavier reached out and touched the head wound she had. She cringed and pulled back from his hand after he applied slight pressure to it. Shaking his head, he grabbed her mechanical arm and gave it a once-over. He sighed before long and walked toward the door. "The lab, let's go. I'll patch up your head and repair your arm so you can go on your way again."

"Awfully agreeable today, Xavier," River said after a moment's hesitation. She followed close behind him.

"Just don't feel like arguing today," Xavier's voice was gruff and tired-sounding.

"You probably haven't been getting much sleep now, have you?" River cradled her arm as she struggled to catch up with his fast pace.

"Who has time for sleep these days? The SGPs are becoming awfully organized and keep knocking on our door every day…or so it seems."

River could think of nothing else to say to him the rest of the way to the lab. Something was bothering him, and he was trying somewhat badly to keep it under wraps while speaking with her. *What's bothering him, I wonder? It's not like him to be so prickly.*

They arrived at the lab door, and Xavier immediately ushered her in. River glanced back at him and saw a look of annoyance overtake his face. *Oh, I'm sorry you have to fix me. If you hadn't given me mechanical limbs in the first place, you wouldn't have this issue!* She glared at him as he came to stand in front of her.

"What the hell is your problem?" River asked angrily.

"Just sit down and shut up so I can send you on your way already," Xavier responded coldly.

"Do you honestly think I need you to fix me before I leave?"

"No one else can. Not that anyone could. The invulnerable River. Always got to be out rescuing someone else."

"Damnit, Xavier. Seriously, what the hell is your problem?" River started to tug on her mechanical arm again. *What the hell? It's like I can't control the impulse.* "Why do I keep getting the feeling like I have to scratch my metal arm off? It's starting to drive me nuts."

"You took a blow to the head, River." He sighed. "Look, you're not going to be able to leave for a while. I need to be able to look at your chipset to determine the damage." Xavier attempted to try to move her to his desk.

"No. Not until we can get this resolved. I've never seen you so annoyed before. What happened? Why won't you talk to me?" River grabbed his face with her good hand to force him to look her in the eyes. Xavier sighed heavily and shrugged as if he was signaling defeat.

"I know you look at me as if I'm some kind of mad scientist. And maybe I am to a certain degree. But that doesn't mean that I'm not a human being still, or that I don't feel anything. You, Fish, and Jonathon brought the survivors from the Settler's Camp here in an effort to protect them. Some of them were seriously injured, inside and out."

Xavier pushed River away and turned his back to her. "I couldn't save these two twin girls…they couldn't have been more than maybe seven or eight years old. I tried everything I could think of to help them or to ease their suffering. But there's not much we can do anymore for snake venom. I watched helplessly as those two writhed in pain, calling out for their dead parents to come save them. I sat on the floor and held both of them close to try to give them some kind of comfort by telling them they were going to be all right, even though it was a lie. The venom had already spread across their little bodies. They clung to me with what little strength they had, and with every ragged breath they each took, it tore at my heart. In an act of mercy,

I gave both of them a shot of morphine to spare them a slow painful death. I couldn't tell you how much time had elapsed when they finally passed away. All I know is I sat there for what seemed like an eternity, rocking back and forth while holding their lifeless bodies."

Xavier dropped down to his knees and began to cry. "I've never felt so helpless. With all the technology I've been able to create and help sustain our lives, you'd think I would have been able to engineer some kind of miracle drug to cure them. I should have been able to save them, River. They were so young…" He started to sob uncontrollably.

River felt a large lump in her throat and had a hard time swallowing. Xavier was wracked with guilt; it was evident. River understood exactly what he was feeling and could sympathize. She kneeled down beside him and took him into an embrace as he continued to sob heavily onto her shoulders.

"It's not your fault, Xavier. I know it doesn't feel that way, but it's true. It's not your fault at all. I know me telling you that doesn't make you feel any better, but you are capable of saving so many people out there. You've literally saved my life twice so far, and I know I've gone out of my way just to make sure you're protected. There's no one else in the world that I trust more than you, so when you say there was nothing you could do, I believe you 100 percent."

"They were so young…didn't even get a chance to live yet…"

"Hey, I know, I know. Those two girls deserve to be mourned. However, you shouldn't beat yourself up for the rest of your life because of something you didn't have the means of preventing. If anything, this should give you fuel to help make this world a better place, so that way no one else has to suffer the same or similar fate."

River pulled out of the embrace slightly so she could look at his face. His long hair, normally secured tightly in a hair tie, had fallen over his face. "Okay?" She brushed his hair back and tucked it behind his ears. They locked eyes, and River felt her heart race. Neither of them moved for a moment as they stared into each other's eyes.

Taking the initiative, Xavier cupped her face with both hands and pulled her in for a slow, deep kiss. *Wait, this isn't the time for this. But...I don't want to move away.* She returned his kiss with a more fevered approach and wrapped her hands around his neck before moving them down his back. Xavier wrapped his hands around her waist and pulled her tight against him. Neither of them knew if they were acting on an impulse because of the heat of the moment or because their mutual feelings for each other finally came to culmination. But they decided to make the best of the situation anyhow. Surprisingly enough, Xavier was the first to break away.

"River. This could happen...but I don't think this is the proper time or place, considering..." Xavier stumbled with the words as he caught his breath. "Come on, I need to get you patched up before Fish comes looking for you."

He reluctantly let go of her and walked over to the other side of the lab to grab the box of tools he used for maintenance. River frowned and then sighed as she realized Xavier was right. She straightened out her clothes and regained her composure before sitting down at the desk. Xavier let out air after setting the maintenance box on the desk and taking a seat himself.

They both sat in silence as Xavier worked diligently on her arm, repairing and replacing the parts that had gotten damaged when she blocked the shotgun blast protecting Jonathon. River closed her eyes, trying to collect her thoughts. *That just happened...didn't it? This is a normal response. After all, we're human. Unfortunately, we can't allow this to happen at this time. It's just too dangerous. People can't think logically when their emotions are constantly involved. Xavier knows that. I know that. Okay...I feel like I'm forgetting something here. Probably would be a good idea to distance myself from Xavier for a while after this. I should probably go find Fishy before she comes looking for me. Although, is Xavier going to need to put me under in order to check out my chipset?*

"River."

Does my head need stitches?

"Oh, River darling," a voice was calling out to her.

River snapped her eyes open to find Glorious Fish standing in the lab.

So much for going to look for her after this. Should have known her.

"I see you've been getting some quality time with the good doctor." Glorious Fish tossed a wink her way. Xavier snapped the halves of her arm back together loudly. River almost jumped in her seat.

"Yes, I suppose getting maintenance done is a type of quality time. To what do we owe the pleasure, Fish?" Xavier stood up from his chair and walked back behind River to look at her head wound.

"Honestly, I was exploring and happened to see you two in here. So I decided to say hello…and to thank you. I know it wasn't easy getting those who survived to safety, but I wanted you to know that I appreciate it more than I could ever hope to express." Glorious Fish bowed before River.

"Fish. I'm glad we were able to get them here despite the little hiccups that occurred." River nodded and then proceeded to smile at her, letting her know she understood.

"You really had me worried when I heard you jumped in front of that blast like that. I mean, seriously, who deliberately jumps in front of a shotgun like that? If that idiot had aimed any higher, well…you'd have bigger issues." Glorious Fish fidgeted.

"You mean I'd be dead? Yes, I'm well aware. It was a stupid move on my part, and I had acted without thinking."

"It's not the first time she's done something like that. For whatever reason, she likes to jump into danger to protect someone, valuing their life more than her own," Xavier spoke up as he grabbed a pair of tweezers. He worked diligently with the tweezers, removing the bits of debris and the small fragmented pieces of the shotgun plasma slug that hit her.

"I take it she'll make a full recovery, Frosty?" Glorious Fish smirked.

"Sadly, yes. I'll need to do a minor surgery to replace the chipset in her brain, but other than that, she'll be fine. It's a shame really…nothing seems to keep her down for very long," Xavier said as he got up from his chair.

"Well, well, what do you say to that…bionic woman?"

"Uh…I say, when are you planning to operate on me?" River shot Glorious Fish a look as she began to scratch her metal arm again. Glorious Fish looked at her genuinely puzzled.

"Xavier," River said as she looked between him and her arm.

Xavier picked up a clipboard from his desk and began to scribble feverishly on it.

"Xavier?"

"It'll be a couple hours. I can't take your old one out until I have a new one to replace it with. Otherwise, you won't be able to move your metal bits as easily as you can now. You'll have to tolerate the odd sensations until I can finish the one I'm working on. Or you can detach your arm and go to sleep while I develop you a new chipset. Whichever you prefer," Xavier responded nonchalantly as he picked up a diagram from his desk.

"You sure you can't take out the old chipset right now?" River asked.

"I could, but then it takes me that much longer to develop your chipset." He turned his head toward River. "Why have two operations and waste both of our time when I can just perform one operation later that makes better use of our time?"

Realizing she can't fight his logic, she sighed. "Fine. I'll go lie down for a while."

"Sleep well, River. I can only imagine the many things we'll have to discuss later," Glorious Fish said as she placed a hand on River's back. "Once again, thank you for getting my people out of there." She left the room immediately afterward.

31

"Hey, Xavier?" Jonathon yelled as he knocked on the lab door. "Are you there?"

"Stop shouting and just open the door already!" Xavier's aggravated voice yelled within the room.

Jonathon opened the door and walked inside. He found Xavier in the corner of the room, bent over a small metallic table with a number of contraptions and gadgets surrounding him and the top of his head. He didn't bother to look up from what he was doing as Jonathon came to stand next to him.

"Xavier? Hi, I'm Jonathon Richtor—"

"I know who you are. You're the guy River took a bullet for." Xavier peered up at Jonathon briefly. "I really don't need to know why, or if there was any history between the two of you. Just state your purpose." He turned his gaze back to the table.

Awfully direct.

"Right. So I've been looking for a medicine called Cipraline for my sister Madison. However, it seems damn near impossible to find these days. River mentioned that you might be able to manufacture a cure that would rid my little sister of the autoimmune disease she's been struggling with." Jonathon tucked his hands behind his back.

Silence filled the room. Xavier readjusted the magnifying scope on his headgear before going back to his tinkering. Several minutes passed, and still nothing was said. *Is it possible he just didn't hear me? Too absorbed into whatever he's...creating?*

Jonathon reached out a hand and placed it on Xavier's shoulder, hoping it would grab his attention. "Xavier..."

"Mr. Richtor, before I agree to anything with regard to my abilities or if I'll even help you, I'd appreciate it if you weren't so timid with me. I know what type of man you are, and I consider it beneath you to try to play on heartstrings that don't exist. Try again."

Jonathon hung his head down and silently laughed to himself. He wasn't expecting that type of response from him. *Do I honestly still come off as a reporter? It's not like I'm trying to dig for information anymore these days. I'll be directly up front to him then.* He cleared his throat.

"Sorry. I'm not here to play timid with you in hopes of you helping me out. But it is the truth that I need your help. I'm desperate. I didn't navigate through the SGP warzone and underground with a group of people I've never met before for nothing. Now is there any way...you can either manufacture a cure or at least get me some Cipraline I can deliver to my sister?"

Xavier finished up working on the chipset in front of him and set it aside. He spun around in his chair to look at Jonathon.

"Your sister. You said her name was Madison, correct? Where is she at this moment?"

"She's with...my other sister and brother in-law. Claire and Brad Jamesson," Jonathon said hesitantly.

"Ah...well, that just shortened down my workload tremendously. Mind you, the current situation is only temporary. There will be a more permanent solution down the line." Xavier crossed the lab to his desk.

"What are you talking about? Do you know something I don't?" Jonathon asked, confused.

"Mr. Richtor, I know plenty of things that you don't. But in this particular regard, there is something. It's easier to show you rather than explain it. Here!" Xavier tossed his Tilithe triangle to Jonathon. "You can talk to the Jamessons through that. They'll fill you in. Now if you'll excuse me, I have surgery I need to perform on one of my favorite subjects."

Xavier raced out of the room, a gigantic grin plastered on his face. Jonathon stared at the doorway, puzzled, before shifting his gaze back to the Tilithe triangle in his hands. *So Xavier knows my sister and brother-in-law, huh? This is a rather happy coincidence.* He flipped the Tilithe up in the air before catching it and placing it on the table Xavier was previously working at.

"All right, so what's the code word to reach the Jamessons?" Jonathon thought aloud as he flipped the top of the Tilithe back. "Is it Claire?"

The Tilithe did nothing.

"How about Brad? Or Bradford?"

The Tilithe still did not react. Jonathon scratched the back of his head wondering what name to try next. *It can't be under Madison. Oh! I know.*

"Jamesson."

The Tilithe hummed and then began to chirp as it attempted to reach its designated patron. One full minute passed before someone picked up.

"Yes, Dr. Frost?" Brad's face appeared over the holographic space.

"No, it's me, Brad. Jonathon," Jonathon said as he leaned closer to the Tilithe.

"Jonathon? What—wait. Where's Dr. Frost?"

"Dr. Frost? Oh you mean—right. He's in the middle of conducting surgery right now. He handed me the Tilithe so I could contact you guys. How's Madison doing?" Jonathon felt anxious.

Brad turned his face away for a moment as he spoke to whomever was next to him before returning his attention back to Jonathon.

"She's doing quite well." He sighed. "Did you want to speak with her?" Brad asked, impatient.

"Please. If I could."

"Yeah, that's fine. I sent Claire to go get her. Matter of fact, here she is." Brad immediately handed over the Tilithe after he was finished speaking.

Madison's strawberry-blonde hair filled the holographic space before she pulled the Tilithe away from her face. Jonathon couldn't believe it was her staring back at him. Her face appeared much fuller and vibrant of color compared to when he had seen her last.

"Madison?" Jonathon asked, incredulous.

"Jon! Oh, Jon. Yes, it's me! Look! I'm not so rail skinny anymore," Madison responded excitedly.

"You look better. I don't quite know how to put it into words, but you actually look healthier. What are they feeding you over there?"

"Peas mostly. Which I'm starting to hate the taste of. When are you coming to pick me back up?" Madison asked.

"Soon, hopefully. I still can't believe it. It almost feels like this trip I've taken is all for nothing." Jonathon paused for a second. *Oh right, Xavier said to ask.* "Hey, Madison, would you be able to get either Brad or Claire for me to speak with? The doctor here mentioned they would be able to explain to me what was going on."

Madison tilted her head as she thought to herself. She turned her head as if to catch someone walking by but instead changed her mind and turned back to Jonathon.

"They both disappeared somewhere. But I should be able to explain it to you. They've been doing a lot of explaining to me as they've had to document all the changes I've been going through." Madison shook her head, confident.

Worried the details might be confused, Jonathon was hesitant about having her explain it to him. However, after seeing how confident she felt about explaining it, he decided it couldn't hurt. "All right, by all means, Maddie, explain it to me."

32

You'll never amount to anything. Always crying all the time. Should have just gotten rid of you when I had the chance. You're useless! You hear me, River? You're useless!

River bolted upright. Drenched in sweat and breathing heavily, she touched her face and then felt along her surroundings. *Cold, metallic…table? Phew. Good, I'm still at the base. It was just a nightmare. Relax, River. Come on, shake it off.* Shaking her head to clear it, she swung her legs off the edge and jumped off the table. The soft clank of her right foot on the floor was a small comfort, and she walked across the room to the far wall to turn on the light. The hex lights at the corners of the room illuminated the room slowly. Now that she could see clearly, she realized that Xavier was also there, curled up on the floor with a pillow by the table she was previously lying on.

With the nightmare still fresh in her mind, she bolted back across the room and down onto the floor. River stifled the urge to shake him, the desperate need of wanting to hear his voice growing. She wrapped her arms around her legs as she pulled them to her chest, watching patiently as Xavier's unconscious body continued to breathe in and out. Some time passed before she managed to work up the courage to shake him. Leaning forward, she extended her arm out to touch him but stopped as he began to awake on his own.

As if he was able to sense her sitting next to him, he bounded off the floor and pulled her to her feet before pulling her hastily into his arms. Burying his face into her neck, he squeezed her so tight that tears began to form in River's eyes.

"River. You can't keep doing this to me. The pain, the suffering, the constant worry and concern if you're going to come home."

"I have to, Xavier…"

"Look, I get it. I really do." Xavier said, sighing. "There's something you should know. Before I get into that, I do want to let you know that while you were asleep, I recalibrated both your arm and leg to work more proficiently with the new chipset in your head." He released her and walked across the room to lean against the wall.

"Did something happen while I was asleep?" River looked at him, puzzled.

"Indeed. Although even with you awake, I don't think it would have helped any." Xavier crossed his arms and stared down at the floor in front of him.

"Well? What happened?" River asked, panic starting to swell inside her.

Xavier snapped his head upward and stared at River straight in the face.

"There was an airstrike launched at the Jamessons."

"What? How did they find them? Weren't they underground?" River gasped in horror.

"Not sure. I don't know how accurate this report is though. I overheard on the SGP radio that they were launching an airstrike into their area and that they were going to be specifically looking for them. I tried to get ahold of them beforehand to let them know of the impending attack but no luck."

"So we don't know for sure if they're dead or not, right?"

"The SGP radio reported the entire area was decimated. However, they were unable to find any bodies."

"So there's a chance, right?" River asked, trying to sound hopeful.

Xavier pushed himself off the wall and walked before River. He tucked a strand of her hair behind her ear.

"There's always a chance, dear River. I knew once I told you, you'd be itching to go off and search…so I'm not even going to bother stopping you." He brushed a soft kiss across her forehead. "Go. Go now before I change my mind."

River furrowed her eyebrows as she watched him turn away. He said nothing and did nothing as he left the room. He didn't even look behind him. *My god, it's almost like he doesn't expect me to come back from this one.* River shook her head to banish the thoughts that were forming. *Need to get back to the task at hand.*

River walked to the far end of her room and pulled one of her harmony suits off the wall rack. Feeling the texture of the suit in between her fingers brought back memories of the day she designed the prototype. She chuckled to herself as she began to put it on and readjust all the straps to contour the suit to her body. The prototype was a total disaster as she called it. It did nothing for her or for her performance. It was literally a nuisance and did more harm than good. Xavier had to cut her out of it as the compression mechanisms inside the carbon fibers started to cut off circulation to all of her limbs.

Three working designs later, she had her full body harmony suit capable of not only forming to her body, but also allowing her to always operate at the highest capacity. It opened up and regulated blood flow throughout her entire body, allowing her to move and react faster than normal.

After verifying that all the straps were properly adjusted, she locked the brackets together for her mechanical limbs and began to rotate them to make sure they were correctly in place. Satisfied, she scooped up a belt of ammo and an MP5 and proceeded to leave the room.

There's no way in hell I'm dying out there. Just you watch, Xavier—I'll be back.

33

"Xavier, it appears the SGP report was correct," River said as she connected to Xavier over the Tilithe. "There is absolutely nothing here. It's just a giant crater."

Xavier leaned back in his chair, rubbing his temples. *What a nightmare. The last few years of experiments and research destroyed within a matter of minutes. Tch.*

"You're positive that there's nothing there?" he asked, wanting to make sure.

"It's completely destroyed, Xavier. There's not even a single remnant or shred of evidence that something was here to begin with," River responded angrily.

"All right, all right. Now you said there's nothing but a crater, but can you tell how deep the crater is, by any chance?"

"Crater may not be the correct operative word here…giant hole isn't either. Let's just say it's much, much bigger than a crater," River said as she continued to look around.

"Okay, since measuring the area affected is obviously out of the question, what exactly are you suggesting?" Xavier's interest was piqued.

"I'm suggesting multiple bombs. Some kind of carpet bombing. Or at least something akin to a gigantic shovel. There's multiple craters here that stretch for a few miles."

"What the—multiple craters? Then how can you be sure that you're at the location of what used to be their residence?"

River went silent. Xavier smirked as he watched her face mull over the possibility. *Perhaps all is not lost after all. Well, I'm not a betting man. The research is long gone, but the Jamessons may live to see another day.*

"Xavier? Hang on a sec…" River's voice came across, barely higher than a whisper, the sounds of foot stomps and crunching of dirt almost overpowering her voice. She dropped the Tilithe suddenly, her face completely disappearing from view. Xavier leaned forward in his chair.

"River?"

No response. He peered closer to the Tilithe, looking for some kind of clue or shadow as to what was happening. After several moments of silence passed by, the sound of metal on metal perforated the air. Xavier swallowed hard as panic started to set in. He hoped River didn't run into one of the mechanized units Glorious Fish was telling him about earlier. His fears were lifted as a katana clamored to the ground in front of the Tilithe. *What the? How primitive. Who still uses swords in this age?* he thought.

A mix of grunts and heavy breathing filled the air next. River rolled on the ground, grabbing the Tilithe as she went. As she stood up, the Tilithe captured the emptiness of the crater she had been talking about and a familiar tall man with long brown hair. His gray eyes were narrow and unforgiving as he shifted his gaze between River and the object in her hands.

"You're not going to believe this, Xavier," River said. "Look who I found."

"Well, I'll be," Xavier said, surprised. "It's the Jamesson's assistant. Tempest, was it?"

"It is," the man responded, breathing heavily. His eyes focused on River. "Mr. Frost, who is this woman?"

Xavier raised an eyebrow. *That's peculiar.* "Tempest, do you not remember River?"

Sundered

Tempest switched his gaze from River to the Tilithe again before returning to River. He widened his eyes before narrowing them again, as if he was trying to access a long-distance memory.

"Ms. Rutherford?" Tempest asked, confused.

"Yeah, it's me, Tempest," River answered.

"Forgive me," Tempest said, dropping down to the ground on a knee. "I did not recognize you."

"That's an understatement. You came at me as if I was the one responsible for this mess."

"My apologies, Ms. Rutherford. I was blinded with rage. I was searching desperately for the Jamessons and Ms. Madison. And well, you look nothing like you did the last time I've seen you."

Xavier could make out the sound of a smack on skin above the Tilithe. He grinned as he realized River must have face-palmed herself. Those who haven't seen River in the past few years could barely recognize her, thanks to her drastic hair job and hardcore wardrobe attire. The changes, while they helped her elude the SGP forces, still left her allies baffled. Yet she still expected her allies to automatically know who she was. Just as she was expecting with Tempest now.

"All right, all right. So Tempest, what happened here? Do you have any idea?" Xavier said, readjusting in his chair. He began to hear footsteps coming down from the hall, so he spun in his chair to face the door.

"Sadly, I do not. I was in the middle of preparing for a trip to Arcturus when I heard air-raid sirens. By the time I turned around, I was slammed into the side of the car. When I finally came to, it was several hours later, and the landscape was as you see now," Tempest said.

Xavier turned his attention back to the Tilithe holographic space briefly before turning his head back toward the doorway. Jonathon came walking in through the doorway, whistling. Xavier shook his head and put a finger to his lips. Jonathon instantly stopped whistling and bit down on his lips.

"Do you know how large the crater is, by any chance?" River asked. "I imagine it must be a few miles."

"A few, yes. I walked for a while earlier and made it to one end. I found no signs or remnants of the Jamessons or the young Madison anywhere. It's almost like they were vaporized," Tempest responded.

"What!" Jonathon shouted, alarmed at what he heard.

"Who's there now?" River asked, turning the Tilithe toward her face.

"River, slight problem. Okay, maybe it's a problem that qualifies as more than just slight. Jonathon just walked in," Xavier said, watching Jonathon's expressions.

"Where are you? Where are they? What happened?" Jonathon asked, hysterical.

"Here we go," Xavier said, muttering under his breath.

"Well? Can anyone explain?" Jonathon got louder and louder as he continued to ask questions.

River rubbed her arm and cleared her throat as she began to look down at the ground. Xavier continued to stare at Jonathon as his state of mind began to visibly deteriorate right in front of him.

"Jonathon… listen, you're gonna want to sit down. This isn't going to be easy to hear." River voice was soft and calm.

Jonathon's mouth dropped, and his eyes grew wide. "What happened? Just tell me."

"Jon—"

"No! Don't tell me to calm down," Jonathon said, interrupting her.

"Jonathon, please."

"River, seriously. This is going to drive me nuts."

"Jon, they're gone," River said flatly. "Are you happy now? Know what else? Everything that they were is gone. *Gone*, Jon. The whole area."

"No…it can't be." Jonathon's eyes began to water.

"It is, Jon, and since you wanted to know so badly, you're gonna have to face it." No emotion registered on River's face. She was completely blank.

"Damnit, River, when did you become such a coldhearted bitch?"

"Since the government decided it didn't need good or softhearted individuals anymore. That's when." River looked away from the Tilithe. "Xavier, Tempest and I will travel back to the Axler in a bit. We're gonna survey the area for a little longer to see if we can find any possible clues." She ended the connection.

34

"Jon, I'm not the best individual to speak with in regards to mourning. But you need to understand something. She's suffering just as badly as you are. You think it's easy having to relay information like this?" Xavier said, leaning back in his chair.

"No, but at the very least, she could tried harder. For god sakes, I'm not a stranger to that woman, and yet she continues to treat me like one. Why is she so cold? What did I do to her?" Jonathon said bitterly.

"You call her cold, but you really don't understand anything, do you? That *cold* woman fights more fiercely than anyone else I know, loves life with all she's got, and protects what she can with everything she is. She knows she can't save them all, but that don't stop her from trying. She's not selective. You've seen her body, haven't you? She didn't get those mechanical limbs by ignoring those in need. What you call being *coldhearted* is just a woman trying to keep her sanity intact as she continues to take on the world," Xavier said defensively.

"Shutting yourself off from the world is just the same as being cold."

"Jonathon, you may have seen your fair share of travesties, but that doesn't mean you understand how she feels. That woman, that strong, selfless woman, is in pain every day…constantly. I've had the displeasure of seeing her cry once, and let me tell you, it was one of the saddest things I've ever seen. It broke my heart to watch her cry in agony because she failed to protect someone. She risks her body and her well-being on so little just to help people. You...you would never understand that. That cold woman...is one of the strongest individuals I've ever met. Besides, you shouldn't have even walked in while we were having that conversation. River wanted to confirm the intel we received before coming to talk to you anyhow."

Jonathon stared at Xavier's face. He knew he was letting his emotions get the better of him, but he didn't know what else to do. Life for the past ten years hadn't been easy, and the loss of the one person he had done nothing but care for was particularly mind-numbing. In an effort to keep going, Jonathon had tried desperately to smother any emotions he'd been feeling as he feared the guilt would be too much for him to handle. He envied River for how she strived to push forward regardless of what the current circumstances were. She still had a purpose, something she absolutely felt was worth dying for. His reasons for living were taken from him. He didn't even notice that Xavier had left the room.

The words that Xavier spoke to him still echoed in his head, and the guilt from the loss of Madison caused him to drop to his knees. He couldn't hold it in anymore. Jonathon hung his head low as the tears began to bead from his eyes and roll down his cheeks. The tears fell silently, forming tiny puddles on the metal floor of the lab room. Rage began to rise inside as the guilt he felt began to overtake him. He lashed out at the tear puddles on the floor before clawing at himself. The pain did nothing to distance him from the agony, however, and he started to scream.

He rolled onto the floor and curled into a ball, rocking back and forth, as sorrow took over his entire being. Jonathon didn't know what to do with himself. He felt himself become more and more despondent and continued to stay curled up on the floor, hoping death would come for him. He shut his eyes for just a moment and then opened them to find a pair of blood-covered combat boots in front of him. He turned his head upward so he could see who was standing there. It was Glorious Fish.

"You need to get up. Right now," Glorious Fish said, glaring at him.

"Leave me alone. You couldn't possibly understand how I feel right now."

In one swift movement, Glorious Fish angrily grabbed him and pulled him up to his feet. "I WOULDN'T UNDERSTAND? I WOULDN'T UNDERSTAND!" she screamed at his face. "Almost all of my people are dead! *Dead.* Do you hear me? After several long years of keeping them safe, most of them were taken in an instant! You're not the only one suffering from the losses here. Stop feeling sorry for yourself."

Glorious Fish dropped him, her hands visibly shaking. Jonathon fell to his knees again and slouched.

"What do you want from me?" Jonathon said quietly. "The last remaining loved ones I had were just taken from me. Am I not to mourn their deaths?"

Glorious Fish just stood there before him, silent. Her chest rose and fell with heavy breaths.

After not receiving an answer from Glorious Fish, Jonathon stared up at her and slowly climbed to his feet. "How am I supposed to feel? Tell me, Glorious Fish. Ceresa Andrews. Whatever it is you call yourself. WHAT AM I SUPPOSED TO DO!" Jonathon clenched the front of Glorious Fish's jacket and leaned forward as he spoke to her.

In retaliation, she slapped him with the back of her hand. Jonathon fell backward, releasing his grip immediately.

"You need…to go take care of your son," Glorious Fish said as she turned her head.

"My son? My son? Is this a cruel joke? My son's been missing for the past couple years. I don't even know if he's still alive,"

Jonathon said as he walked toward Glorious Fish and stared at her angrily.

"He *was* missing. I found him while I was covering you guys' escape from the caravan. He's alive, Jon, and he desperately needs you." Glorious Fish turned away from Jonathon completely and walked toward the door. For a second there, Jonathon thought he saw tears forming in her eyes.

"He's...alive? Where is he?" Jonathon said as he followed her.

"Matthew is currently sleeping in the second exam room," Glorious Fish said over her shoulder before turning down the hallway. Tension was evident in every part of her body.

Jonathon stood at the doorway for an extra few minutes. *Matthew...my son...my son! He's alive? He's alive! I need...I need to go see him quickly.*

Not wanting to waste any more time, Jonathon started running down the hallway.

35

Lub-dub. Lub-dub.

Jonathon could feel his heart beat hard in his chest as he slowly approached the exam room door. He was both anxious and terrified about what he was going to find behind it. A tingle of guilt was also beginning to wash over him as he realized he had been putting in far more effort in taking care of Madison than he ever did looking for his son. *He's always been a strong boy. Obedient. Resourceful. Dependable. Never complained when it came to having to move around or helping me look after Madison. Oh god.*

He backed away from the door and hung his head, tears streaming down his face. *I can't see him. I don't deserve to see him after I've basically abandoned him. What kind of father am I? A shitty one. Come on, Jonathon, get it together. You'll be worse than a shitty father if you can't muster the courage to see him now. He needs you.* MOVE.

Drying the tears from his face, Jonathon breathed in deeply to prepare himself. Exhaling, he reached his left hand to the door handle and was about to open it when the door next to him opened. It was Xavier exiting. Staring down at his cybernetic clipboard, he walked forward and bumped into Jonathon. He looked up at Jonathon, surprised.

"Mr. Richtor. I would have thought you'd still be in my lab, mourning. What brings you down this corridor? Are you here to see George? I wouldn't recommend it. It's not pretty. I was able to put some of my good skills to use earlier by stopping the bleeding, but he's still got a long road to recovery. With the sedative I gave him though, he should sleep pretty good."

Jonathon blinked rapidly, processing the information, his left hand still on the door handle. Noticing Jonathon's hand, Xavier nodded.

"Ah, you must be here to see this young man. I believe Fish said his name was Matthew. He's in pretty rough shape himself. If you're going in to see him, I'll be following you. I need to check his IVs," Xavier said as he slid his fingers across the clipboard, causing Matthew's chart information to be displayed.

Jonathon lingered for a few seconds longer before facing the door and opening it. *Here goes nothing...Please, please be all right, Matthew.* Upon walking inside, he stepped out of the way to allow Xavier to follow suit inside.

"He's over there," Xavier said, pointing to the back corner of the room where a bed and IV rack were set up. "Ah, Matthew. I see you're awake finally. Don't mind me. I'm just here to swap out your IV bags. You do have a visitor though."

"Who...who's there?" a weak voice called out.

Jonathon felt a large lump in his throat and swallowed hard.

"It's me...Matt," Jonathon said, trying hard to keep from weeping. Relief and concern began to overwhelm him, and he almost lost it completely.

"Dad?" Matthew asked as he struggled to try to pull himself upright.

"Yeah, buddy," Jonathon responded as he walked to the side of the bed. He watched as Xavier adjusted a pillow under Matthew's head and helped pull him up so he could lean back against the wall.

Jonathon couldn't help but gasp as he saw Matthew's frail state. Matthew was so bone thin, Jonathon thought he could snap in two at any given moment. Outside the two IV lines running in both of his hands, Matthew also had numerous cuts and bruises all over his body. It was almost like he had been tortured and starved the entire time he'd been missing. The sight of him made Jonathon feel sick to his stomach and even guiltier than he did before.

"I'm sorry, buddy," Jonathon said in between tears. "I'm so, so sorry."

Matthew extended one of his bony hands toward Jonathon, tears also forming in his eyes.

"Dad…it's okay. It's not your fault…"

"But it is my fault. If I had been the one fishing that day then you'd…you'd…" Jonathon couldn't finish his sentence as he fell to his knees and leaned forward into the bed.

"Dad. Please. It's okay…I had too…to keep them…away," Matthew said in a low voice as he drifted off to sleep, his body slumping to the side.

"Oh my god! Matthew?" Jonathon practically shouted as he jumped to his feet.

"Quiet, Mr. Richtor. He's fine. Or at least he will be as his body heals more. If you hadn't noticed, just that bit of movement was enough to exhaust him, so he ended up passing out. Like I told you outside, he's in rough shape," Xavier said, pulling Jonathon outside.

"But he will heal, right?"

"Depends on him." Xavier stopped for a moment as he saw Jonathon's eyes grow wide. "Relax. I see no reason why he won't recover. Trust me, I did a very thorough exam. He's dehydrated, undernourished, and has a few wounds that haven't healed properly, but it's nothing I can't treat. He's a strong kid. He'll pull through. To help speed it along a little, I've been administering synthetic vitamins in with his fluids. You should see significant improvement out of him within a week or so." Xavier patted him on the shoulder.

Sundered

Jonathon stared at Xavier for a little bit, his emotions still running rather high. His faced twitched as he struggled with himself to regain his composure, but after a few minutes, he was able to nod to Xavier to show he understood.

"Good. Now, Mr. Richtor, I expect you to control yourself in there. I can't say I've ever experienced what you're going through right now. At least in the respect of being a father, but I have experienced what it feels like to see a loved one in such a state. I assure you, it's going to get better. Because if it doesn't, River will have my ass in a sling. Nobody wants that, trust me. How else will anyone get their medical needs taken care of?" Xavier smirked, his eyes warm.

Jonathon found himself laughing as he realized Xavier was trying to lighten the mood and even going so far as to show him some compassion. It was totally unexpected, but it went to show that even the zaniest of doctors were capable of normal human interaction.

"You're right. We wouldn't want that...thanks, Xavier," Jonathon said, extending his hand forward.

"You're welcome," Xavier said, returning the handshake. He nodded to himself before patting Jonathon on the back as he passed by him.

Jonathon watched Xavier as he walked down the hall. *It seems I read Xavier entirely the wrong way before. He, like River and Ceresa, do their best to keep their feelings under wraps, not to protect themselves, but so they can protect those around them. No one is capable of much rational thought under emotional duress, myself included.*

"Jon!"

"Uh, yeah, Xavier?" Jonathon said, jumping a little.

"Stop watching me and go watch over your son already. He needs you." Xavier tsk-tsked before walking around the corner.

Jonathon turned around and reopened the door to the exam room. Matthew was still slumped over in his bed. Jonathon blew air out his cheeks to help settle his nerves. *It'll be okay. I know it's going to be hard, but I have to stay strong for Matthew's sake. Madison wouldn't want me to lose face even with her loss. She'd want me to live on, head held high. Hopefully, when we can get a chance, I can prepare some kind of funeral service for her,* Jonathon thought awhile as he carefully lifted and maneuvered Matthew's body back underneath the covers and laid the pillow back underneath his head.

Eyeing a chair on the other side of the room, Jonathon picked it up and brought it to Matthew's bedside so he could sit on it. He watched Matthew sleep for a while, observing his face. It appeared peaceful and relaxed, as if the very dreams he was having brought him tremendous comfort.

Jonathon leaned forward in his chair and used his right hand to move the hair out of Matthew's face, speaking aloud as he did so. "It's all right, Matthew. I'm here for you. I won't lie to you. Part of me wants to be looking for Madison and Claire and Brad as I want to believe they're still alive. But I can't do that right now. Do you know why? Because you're my son, Matthew, and this time, I want to protect you."

36

Bzzert. Bzzert. Bzzert.

A tall middle-aged man with short neatly kept hair didn't even bother to look up from his computer as he answered his cell phone.

"Alexander," he answered promptly.

"Alex, do they expect anything at all?" a female husky voice came on the line.

"Not even in the slightest, Ms. White."

"And the Blood Singer, he's made it into the base?"

"Yes, Ms. White. It'll only take ten minutes for the uplink to send the command. Just awaiting your order."

A soft seductive laugh could be heard from over the phone.

"Excellent. I expect nothing less."

"Of course, Ms. White. I am but a humble servant that aims to please."

"If that's the case, Alex, why must I ask you every day to call me by my title?"

"My apologies, Madam Secretary."

"Consider this the last time I make the request."

"Yes, Madam Secretary."

"And the airstrike on the Jamessons' residence?"

"Went off without a hitch. The entire area and its surroundings have been decimated. There's nothing left there. Except for the dozen or so craters of course."

"Bravo," the woman said, followed by the sound of clapping.

"One of our drones picked up something though. It seems the former security courier, River Rutherford, is still alive. She was spotted investigating the crater with an unknown male accomplice."

"That is...unfortunate."

"What are your orders, Madam Secretary?" Alexander asked.

"Activate the Blood Singer."

"Right away, Madam Secretary."

With that said, Alexander dropped his cell phone to the floor and slid across the room with his chair. He stopped in front of another computer, hooked up to six monitors and various cords and wires, and proceeded to peck hastily at the keyboard. Line after line of text appeared on screen and disappeared with each new window that opened. Several minutes passed by before Alexander was finished. He leaned back in his chair, a smug look on his face.

"And with this final stroke, the Blood Singer—will sing!" He laughed aloud as he leaned forward and, with his index finger, pressed the Enter key.